Danger in Deep Space

Carey Rockwell

Illustrator: Louis Glanzman

Contents

DANGER IN DEEP SPACE

BY

Carey Rockwell

Illustrator: Louis Glanzman

DANGER IN DEEP SPACE

THE TOM CORBETT
SPACE CADET STORIES

By Carey Rockwell

STAND BY FOR MARS!
DANGER IN DEEP SPACE

[Illustration]

A TOM CORBETT Space Cadet Adventure

DANGER IN
DEEP SPACE

By CAREY ROCKWELL

WILLY LEY Technical Adviser

GROSSET & DUNLAP *Publishers* New York

Illustrations by
LOUIS GLANZMAN

CHAPTER 1

Stand by to reduce thrust on main drive rockets!" The tall, broad-shouldered officer in the uniform of the Solar Guard snapped out the order as he watched the telescanner screen and saw the Western Hemisphere of Earth looming larger and larger.

"Aye, aye, Captain Strong," replied a handsome curly-haired Space Cadet. He turned to the ship's intercom and spoke quickly into the microphone.

"Control deck to power deck. Check in!"

"Power deck, aye," a bull-throated voice bellowed over the loud-speaker.

"Stand by rockets, Astro! We're coming in for a landing."

"Standing by!"

The Solar Guard officer turned away from the telescanner and glanced quickly over the illuminated banks of indicators on the control panel. "Is our orbit to Space Academy clear?" he asked the cadet. "Have we been assigned a landing ramp?"

"I'll check topside, sir," answered the cadet, turning back to the intercom. "Control deck to radar deck. Check in!"

"Radar bridge, aye," drawled a lazy voice over the speaker.

"Are we cleared for landing, Roger?"

"Everything clear as glass ahead, Tom," was the calm reply.

"We're steady on orbit and we touch down on ramp seven. Then"—the voice began to quicken with excitement—"three weeks' liberty coming up!"

The rumbling voice of the power-deck cadet suddenly broke in over the intercom. "Lay off that space gas, Manning. Just see that this space wagon gets on the ground in one piece. Then you can dream about your leave!"

"Plug your jets, you big Venusian ape man," was the reply, "or I'll turn you inside out!"

"Yeah? You and what fleet of spaceships?"

"Just me, buster, with my bare hands!"

The Solar Guard officer on the control deck smiled at the young cadet beside him as the good-natured argument crackled over the intercom speaker overhead. "Looks like those two will never stop battling, Corbett," he commented dryly.

"Guess they'll never learn, sir," sighed the cadet.

"That's all right. It's when they stop battling that I'll start getting worried," answered the officer. He turned back to the controls. "One hundred thousand feet from Earth's surface! Begin landing procedure!"

As Cadet Tom Corbett snapped orders into the intercom and his unit-mates responded by smooth co-ordinated action, the giant rocket cruiser *Polaris* slowly arched through Earth's atmosphere, first nosing up to lose speed and then settling tailfirst toward its destination—the spaceport at Space Academy, U.S.A.

Far below, on the grounds of the Academy, cadets wearing the green uniforms of first-year Earthworms and the blue of the upper-classmen stopped all activity as they heard the blasting of the braking rockets high in the heavens. They stared enviously into the sky, watching the smooth steel-hulled spaceship drop toward the concrete ramp area of the spaceport, three miles away.

In his office at the top of the gleaming Tower of Galileo, Commander Walters, commandant of Space Academy, paused for a moment from his duties and turned from his desk to watch the touchdown of the great spaceship. And on the grassy quadrangle, Warrant Officer Mike McKenny, short and stubby in his scarlet uniform of the enlisted Solar Guard, stopped his frustrating task of drilling newly arrived cadets to watch the mighty ship come to Earth.

Young and old, the feeling of belonging to the great fleet that patrolled the space lanes across the millions of miles of the solar system was something that never died in a true spaceman. The green-clad cadets dreamed of the future when they would feel the bucking rockets in their backs. And the older men smiled faintly as memories of their own first space flight came to mind.

Aboard the *Polaris*, the young cadet crew worked swiftly and smoothly to bring their ship to a safe landing. There was Tom Corbett, an average young man in this age of science, who had been selected as the control-deck and command cadet of the *Polaris* unit after rigid examinations and tests.

SPACE ACADEMY U.S.A.

Topside, on the radar bridge, was Roger Manning, cocky and brash, but a specialist in radar and communications. Below, on the power deck, was Astro, a colonial from Venus, who had been accused of cutting his teeth on an atomic rocket motor, so great was his skill with the mighty "thrust buckets," as he lovingly called the atomic rockets.

Now, returning from a routine training flight that had taken them to the moons of Jupiter, the three cadets, Corbett, Manning, and Astro, and their unit skipper, Captain Steve Strong, completed the delicate task of setting the great ship down on the Academy spaceport.

"Closing in fast, sir," announced Tom, his attention focused on the meters and dials in front of him. "Five hundred feet to touchdown."

"Full braking thrust!" snapped Strong crisply.

Deep inside the *Polaris*, braking rockets roared with unceasing power, and the mighty spaceship eased itself to the concrete surface of the Academy spaceport.

"Touchdown!" yelled Tom. He quickly closed the master control lever, cutting all power, and sudden silence filled the ship. He stood up and faced Strong, saluting smartly.

"Rocket cruiser *Polaris* completes mission"—he glanced at the astral chronometer on the panel board—"at fifteen thirty-three, sir."

"Very well, Corbett," replied Strong, returning the salute. "Check the *Polaris* from radar mast to exhaust ports right away."

"Yes, sir," was Tom's automatic answer, and then he caught himself. "But I thought—"

Strong interrupted him with a wave of his hand. "I know, Corbett, you thought the *Polaris* would be pulled in for a general overhaul and you three would get liberty."

"Yes, sir," replied Tom.

"I'm not sure you won't get it," said Strong, "but I received a message last night from Commander Walters. I think the *Polaris* unit might have another assignment coming up!"

"By the rings of Saturn," drawled Roger from the open hatch to the radar bridge, "you might know the old man would have another mission for us! We haven't had a liberty since we were Earthworms!"

"I'm sorry, Manning," said Strong, "but you know if I had my way, you'd certainly get the liberty. If anyone deserves it, you three do."

By this time Astro had joined the group on the control deck.

"But, sir," ventured Tom, "we've all made plans, I mean—well, my folks are expecting me."

" *Us*, you mean," interrupted Roger. "Astro and I are your guests, remember?"

"Sure, I remember," said Tom, smiling. He turned back to Captain Strong. "We'd appreciate it if you could do something for us, sir. I mean—well, have another unit assigned."

Strong stepped forward and put his arms around the shoulders of Tom and Roger and faced Astro. "I'm afraid you three made a big mistake in becoming the best unit in the Academy. Now every time there's an important assignment to be handed out the name of the *Polaris* unit sticks out like a hot rocket!"

"Some consolation," said Roger dourly.

Strong smiled. "All right, check this wagon and then report to me in my quarters in the morning. You'll have tonight off at least. Unit *dis*-missed!"

The three cadets snapped their backs straight, stood rigid, and saluted as their superior officer strode toward the hatch. His foot on the ladder, he turned and faced them again.

"It's been a fine mission. I want to compliment you on the way you've handled yourselves these past few months. You boys are real spacemen!" He saluted and disappeared down the ladder leading to the exit port.

"And that," said Roger, turning to his unit-mates, "is known as the royal come-on for a dirty detail!"

"Ahhh, stop your gassing, Manning," growled Astro. "Just be sure your radar bridge is O.K. If we do have to blast out of here in a hurry, I want to get where we're supposed to be going!"

"You just worry about the power deck, spaceboy, and let little Roger take care of his own department," replied Roger.

Astro eyed him speculatively. "You know the only reason they allowed this space creep in the Academy, Tom?" asked Astro.

"No, why?" asked Tom, playing along with the game.

"Because they knew any time the *Polaris* ran out of reactant fuel we could just stick Manning in the rocket tubes and have him blow out some of his special brand of space gas!"

"Listen, you Venusian throwback! One more word out of you and—"

"All right, you two!" broke in Tom good-naturedly. "Enough's enough! Come on. We've got just enough time to run up to the mess hall and grab a good meal before we check the ship."

"That's for me," said Astro. "I've been eating those concentrates so long my stomach thinks I've turned into a test tube."

Astro referred to the food taken along on space missions. It was dehydrated and packed in plastic containers to save weight and space. The concentrates never made a satisfactory meal, even though they supplied everything necessary for a healthful diet.

A few moments later the three members of the **Polaris** stood on the main slidewalk, an endless belt of plastic, powered by giant subsurface rollers, being carried from the spaceport to the main academy administration building, the great gleaming Tower of Galileo.

Space Academy, the university of the planets, was set among the low hills of the western part of the North American continent. Here, in the nest of fledgling spacemen, boys from Earth and the colonies of Venus and Mars learned the complex science that would enable them to reach unlimited heights; to rocket through the endless void of space and visit new worlds on distant planets millions of miles from Earth.

This was the year 2353—the age of space! A time when boys dreamed only of becoming Space Cadets at Space Academy, to learn their trade and later enter the mighty Solar Guard, or join the rapidly expanding merchant space service that sent out great fleets of rocket ships daily to every corner of the solar system.

As the slidewalk carried the three cadets between the buildings that surrounded the grassy quadrangle of the Academy, Tom looked up at the Tower of Galileo dominating the entire area.

"You know," he began haltingly, "every time I go near this place I get a lump in my throat!"

"Yeah," breathed Astro, "me too."

Roger made no comment. His eyes were following the path of the giant telescope reflector that moved in a slow arc, getting into position for the coming night's observations. Tom followed his gaze to the massive domed building, housing the giant one-thousand-inch reflector.

"You think we'll ever go as far into the deep with a rocket ship as we can see with the big eye?" he asked.

"I dunno," replied Roger. "That thing can penetrate other star systems in our galaxy. And that's a long way off!"

"Nearest thing to us is Alpha Centauri in our own galaxy, and that's twenty-three and a half million million miles away," commented Astro.

"That's not so far," argued Tom. "Only a few months ago the Solar Alliance sent out a scientific exploration to take a look at that baby."

"Musta been some hop," commented Roger.

"Hey!" cried Tom suddenly. "There's Alfie Higgins!" He pointed in the direction of another slidewalk moving at right angles to their own. The cadet that he singled out on the slidewalk was so thin and small he looked emaciated. He wore glasses and at the moment was absorbed in a paper he held in his hand.

"Well, what do you know!" cried Astro. "The Brain!"

Roger punched Astro in the mid-section. "If you were as smart as he is, you big grease monkey, you'd be O.K."

"Nah!" replied Astro. "If I was as smart as Alfie, I'd be scared. And besides, what do I need to be smart for? I've got you, haven't I?"

When they drew near the other slidewalk, the three members of the *Polaris* unit skipped lightly over and jostled their way past other riders to the slightly built cadet.

"Alfie!" Tom yelled and slapped the cadet on the back. Alfie turned, his glasses knocked askew by Tom's blow, and eyed the three *Polaris* members calmly.

"It gives me great pleasure to view your countenances again, Cadets Corbett, Manning, and Astro," he said solemnly, nodding to each one.

Astro twisted his face into a grimace. "What'd he say, Roger?"

"He's happy to see you," Roger translated.

"Well, in that case," beamed Astro, "I'm happy to see you too, Alfie!"

"What's the latest space dope around the Academy, Alfie?" asked Tom. "What's this?" he indicated the paper in Alfie's hand.

"By the sheerest of coincidences I happen to have a copy of your new assignment!" replied Alfie.

Tom, Roger, and Astro looked at each other in surprise.

"Well, come on, spaceman," urged Roger. "Give us the inside info. Where are we going?"

Alfie tucked the paper in his inside pocket and faced Roger. He cleared his throat and spoke in measured tones. "Manning, I have high regard for your personality, your capabilities, and your knowledge, all of which makes you an outstanding cadet.

But even you know that I occupy a position of trust as cadet courier for Commander Walters and the administrative staff. I am not at liberty to mention anything that I would have occasion to observe while in the presence of Commander Walters or the staff. Therefore, you will please refrain from questioning me any further regarding the contents of these papers!"

Roger's jaw dropped. "Why, you human calculator, you were the one who brought it up in the first place! I oughta knock off that big head of yours!"

Tom and Astro laughed.

"Lay off, Roger," said Tom. "You ought to know Alfie couldn't talk if he wanted to! We'll just have to wait until Captain Strong is ready to tell us what our next assignment will be!"

By this time the slidewalk had carried them to the front of the main dormitory, and the wide doors were crowded with members of the Space Academy Corps heading in for the evening meal. From all corners of the quadrangle, the slidewalks carried Earthworms in their green uniforms, upper-class cadets in deep blue, enlisted spacemen in scarlet red, and Solar Guard officers in their striking uniforms of black and gold. Chatting and laughing, they all were entering the great building.

The *Polaris* unit was well known among other cadet units, and they were greeted heartily from all sides. As Astro and Roger joked with various cadet units, forming up in front of the slidestairs leading down to the mess halls, Alfie turned to take a slidestairs going up. Suddenly he stopped, grabbed Tom by the shoulders, and whispered in his ear. Just as abruptly he turned and raced up the ascending slidestairs.

"What was that about?" asked Roger, as Tom stood staring after the little cadet.

"Roger—he—he said our next assignment would be one of the great experiments in space history. Something to be done that—that hasn't ever been done before!"

"Well, blast my jets!" said Astro. "What do you suppose it is?"

"Ahhh," sneered Roger, "I'll bet it's nothing more than taking some guinea pigs to see how they react to Jovian gravity. That's never been done before either! Why can't we get something exciting for a change?"

Tom laughed. "Come on, you bloodthirsty adventurer, I'm starved!"

But Tom knew that Alfie Higgins didn't get excited easily, and his eyes were wide and his voice trembled when he had whispered his secret to Tom.

The *Polaris* unit was due to embark on a great new adventure!

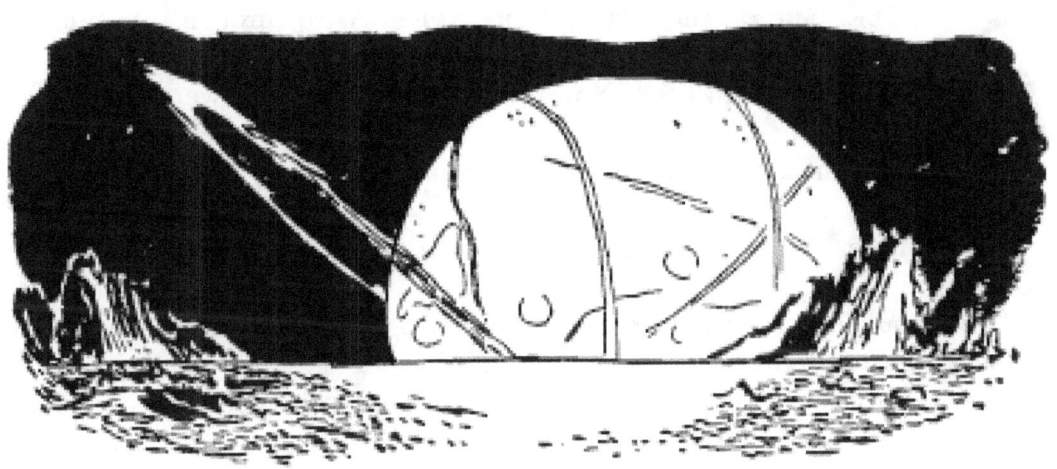

CHAPTER 2

"All O.K. here on the relay circuit," yelled Astro through the intercom from the power deck.

"O.K.," answered Tom. "Now try out the automatic blowers for the main tubes!"

"Wanta give me a little juice for the radar antenna, Astro?" called Roger from the radar deck.

"In a minute, Manning, in a minute," growled Astro. "Only got two hands, you know."

"You should learn to use your feet," quipped Roger. "Any normal Venusian can do just as much with his toes as he can with his fingers!"

Back and forth the bantering had gone for twelve hours, while the three members of the *Polaris* unit tested, checked, adjusted, and rechecked the many different circuits, relays, junction boxes, and terminals in the miles of delicate wiring woven through the ship. Now, as dawn began to creep pink and gray over the eastern horizon, they made their last-minute search through the cavernous spaceship for any doubtful connections. Satisfied there were none, the three weary cadets assembled on the control deck and sipped the hot tea that Manning had thoughtfully prepared.

"You know, by the time we get out of the Academy I don't think there'll be a single *inch* of this space wagon that I haven't inspected with my nose," commented Roger in a tired voice.

"You know you love it, Manning," said Astro, who, though as tired as Tom and Roger, could still continue to work if necessary. His love for the mighty atomic rocket motors, and his ability to repair anything mechanical, was already a legend around the Academy.

The three weary cadets assembled on the control deck

He cared for the power deck of the *Polaris* as if it were a baby.

"Might as well pack in and grab some sleep before we report to Captain Strong," said Tom. "He might have us blasting off right away, and I, for one, would like to sleep and sleep and then sleep some more!"

"I've been thinking about what Alfie had to say," said Roger. "You know, about this being a great adventure."

"What about it?" asked Astro.

"Well, you don't give this kind of overhaul for just a plain, short hop upstairs."

"You think it might be something deeper?" asked Astro softly.

"Whatever it is," said Tom, getting up, "we'll need sleep." He rose, stretched, and walked wearily to the exit port. Astro and Roger followed him out, and once again they boarded the slidewalk for the trip back to the main dormitory and their quarters on the forty-second floor. A half hour later the three members of the *Polaris* were sound asleep.

Early morning found Captain Steve Strong in his quarters, standing at the window and staring blankly out over the quadrangle. In his left hand he clutched a sheaf of papers. He had just reread, for the fifth time, a petition for reinstatement of space papers for Al Mason and Bill Loring. It wasn't easy, as Strong well knew, to deprive a man of his right to blast off and rocket through space, and the papers in question, issued only by the Solar Guard, comprised the only legal license to blast off.

Originally issued as a means of preventing overzealous Earthmen from blasting off without the proper training or necessary physical condition, which resulted in many deaths, space papers had gradually become the only effective means of controlling the vast expanding force of men who made space flight their life's work. With the establishment of the Spaceman's Code a hundred years before, firm rules and regulations for space flight had been instituted. Disobedience to any part of the code was punishable by suspension of papers and forfeiture of the right to blast off.

One of these rules stated that a spaceman was forbidden to blast off without authorization or clearance for a free orbit from a central traffic control. Bill Loring and Al Mason were guilty of having broken the regulation. Members of the crew of the recent expedition to Tara, a planet in orbit around the sun star Alpha Centauri, they had taken a rocket scout and blasted off without permission from Major Connel, the commander of the mission, who, in this case, was authorized traffic-control officer. Connel had recommended immediate suspension of their space papers. Mason and Loring had petitioned for a review, and, to assure impartial judgment, Commander Walters had sent the petition to one of his other officers to make a decision. The petition had landed on Strong's desk.

Strong read the petition again and shook his head. The facts were too clear. There had been flagrant disregard for the rules and there was no evidence to support the suspended spacemen's charge that they had been unjustly accused by Connel. Strong's duty was clear. He had to uphold Major Connel's action and suspend the men for a year.

Once the decision was made, Strong put the problem out of his mind. He walked to his huge circular desk and began sorting through the day's orders and reports. On the top of the pile of papers was a sealed envelope, bordered in red and marked "classified." It was from Commander Walters' office. Thoughtfully he opened it and read:

> To: CAPTAIN STEVE STRONG: Cadet Supervisor,
> *Polaris* Unit
> Upon receipt of this communication, you are ordered to
> transfer the supervisory authority of the cadet unit
> designated as *POLARIS* unit; i.e., Cadets Tom Corbett, Roger
> Manning, and Astro, and the command of the rocket cruiser
> *Polaris*, to the command and supervisory authority of Major
> Connel for execution of mission as outlined herein:
>
> 1. To test range, life, and general performance of audio
>   communications transmitter, type X21.
> 2. To test the above-mentioned transmitter under conditions of
>   deep space flight.
> 3. This test to take place on the planet Tara, Alpha Centauri.
> This communication and all subsequent information relative to
> above-mentioned mission shall be classified as *topmost
> secret*.
>
> Signed: WALTERS, *Commandant*, Space Academy

"So that's it," he thought. "A hop into deep space for the *Polaris* unit!" He smiled. "The cadets of the *Polaris* unit are in for a little surprise in two ways," he thought. "One from the mission and one from Major Connel!"

He almost laughed out loud as he turned to the small desk teleceiver at his elbow. He pressed a button immediately below the screen and it glowed into life to reveal a young man in the uniform of the enlisted guard.

"Yes, Captain Strong?" he asked.

"Call the cadets of the *Polaris* unit," Strong ordered. "Have them report to me here on the double!"

"Aye, aye, sir."

Strong started to turn the set off, but the enlisted man added, "By the way, sir, Al Mason and Bill Loring are here to see you."

"Oh—well—" Strong hesitated.

"They're quite anxious to know if you've reached any decision regarding their petition for reinstatement."

"Mmm—yes, of course. Very well, send them in."

"Aye, aye, sir."

The teleceiver screen blackened. In a moment the door opposite Strong's desk slid back, and Loring and Mason stepped into the office. They shambled forward and stopped in front of the huge desk, obviously ill at ease.

Strong stood up, holding their petition in his hand, and glanced over it briefly even though he knew its contents by heart. He motioned to near-by chairs. "Sit down, please," he said.

The two spacemen settled themselves uncomfortably on the edge of their chairs and waited expectantly as Strong continued to look at the paper.

Loring finally broke the heavy silence.

"Well, Captain Strong, have you made a decision?" he asked. Loring was a heavy-set man, in his middle forties. He needed a shave, and when he talked, his mouth twisted into an ugly grimace.

"Hope it's in our favor, sir," suggested Mason. He was shorter than Loring and, seated, his feet hardly reached the floor. His eyes darted nervously about the huge room, and he kept rolling a dirty black spaceman's cap in his hands.

"Yes, I've reached a decision," said Strong slowly. He faced the two men and looked at both of them with a steady cold stare. "I've decided to sustain Major Connel's action. You are both grounded for the next twelve months. Earth months!"

"What?" shouted Loring, jumping to his feet. He banged his fist down on the desk and leaned over, his face close to Strong's. "You can't do that to us!"

Captain Strong didn't move. "I can," he said coldly. "And I have."

"But—but—" Mason began to whine. "But space flight is all we know! How will we live?"

Strong sat down and leaned back in his chair to get away from the foul odor of Loring's breath. He stared at the two men.

"You should have thought of that before you stole a rocket scout from the expedition and made an unauthorized flight while on Tara," Strong replied. "You're lucky you're not accused, tried, and convicted of theft of a Solar Guard spaceship!"

"We had permission to take that flight," snarled Loring. "That Major Connel is so blasted space happy he forgot he gave us permission. Then when we came back, he slapped us in the brig!"

"Do you have any proof of that?" asked Strong.

"No! But it's our word against his!" He slammed his hat down on the desk and shook his finger in Strong's face. "You haven't any right to take away our papers just on the say-so of a lousy Solar Guard officer who thinks he's king of the universe!"

"Take your filthy hat off my desk, Loring!" barked Strong. "And watch your language!"

Loring realized he had made a mistake and tried to backtrack. "Well, I apologize for that. But I *don't* apologize for saying he thinks he's—"

"Major Connel has been in the Solar Guard for thirty years," said Strong emphatically. "He's been awarded the Solar Medal three times. No other living spaceman has achieved that! Not even Commander Walters! He rose through the ranks of the enlisted Solar Guard and was commissioned as an officer of the Solar Guard in space during an emergency. He qualifies higher than any other spaceman, and he has never been found to be unjust! He's one of the finest spacemen ever to hit the wide, deep, and high!" Strong stopped, choked for breath, and turned away. It wasn't often he lost his temper, but something had to be said in defense of his fellow officer, and particularly since that officer was Connel. He turned back to face the two spacemen, and his voice was hard and cold again.

"You are hereby suspended from space flight for twelve Earth months. Any further petition for appeal of this decision will be denied!"

"All right! All right, Mr. Big!" snapped Loring. "Does this mean we can't even ride as passengers?"

"No rights under the Universal Bill of Rights of the Solar Alliance have been denied you, except that of actively participating in the flight of a spaceship!"

The signal bell of the teleceiver began to chime softly, and on the desk the teleceiver screen glowed again. "Cadets Corbett, Manning, and Astro are here for their assignments, sir," announced the enlisted man outside.

Loring glared at Strong. "I suppose you're going to send some punk kids out on the next trip to Tara and leave us experienced spacemen to rot on the ground, huh?"

Strong didn't see the door slide open to admit the three cadets who entered quietly. His whole attention was focused on the ugly glaring faces of Bill Loring and Al Mason.

"Get this, Loring!" snapped Strong hotly. "The assignments of the *Polaris* unit, whether it be to Tara or the Moon, has nothing to do with your own breech of conduct. In any case, if they were to be assigned, they'd do a better job than you 'experienced' spacemen who are disrespectful of your superior officers and break regulations! If either of you makes one more crack about the Solar Guard or Space Cadets, or *anything* at all, I'll take you out on the quadrangle and pound some common courtesy into your heads! Now get out!"

"All right, all right—" muttered Loring retreating, but with a sneer on his lips. "We'll meet again, Mr. Bigshot Spaceman!"

"I hope so, Loring. And if we do, I hope you've taken a bath. You even smell bad!"

From the rear of the room came a burst of laughter. Tom, Roger, and Astro, unobserved, had been listening and watching their skipper in action. When Loring and Mason had left the room, they advanced to the desk, came to attention, and saluted.

"*Polaris* unit reporting for duty, sir!" snapped Tom crisply.

"At ease," said Strong. "Did you hear all of that?"

"Yes, sir, skipper!" Roger smiled. "And believe me, you really gave it to those two space bums!"

"Yeah," agreed Astro, "but I don't think even *you* could do much for Loring. He's just born to smell bad!"

"Never mind that," said Strong. "I suppose you heard the part about the assignments?"

The three cadets assumed looks of pure innocence.

"We didn't hear a thing, sir," said Tom.

"You'll make a fine diplomat, Corbett," Strong laughed. "All right, sit down and I'll give it to you straight."

They hastily took seats and waited for their skipper to begin.

"You've been assigned as cadet observers on a mission to test the range of a new long-range audio transmitter." Strong paused, then added significantly, "The test is to take place in deep space."

The three cadets only beamed their enthusiastic approval.

"Tara," continued Strong, "is your destination—a planet like Earth in many respects, in orbit around the sun star Alpha Centauri. You'll take the *Polaris* directly to the Venus space station, where the transmitter has been given primary tests, outfit the *Polaris* for hyperdrive, and blast off!"

"Excuse me, sir," interrupted Tom, "but you say 'you'?"

"I mean," replied Strong, "*you*, in the sense that I won't be going along with you. Oh, don't worry!" said Strong, holding up his hand as a sudden look of anticipation spread over the faces of the three boys. "You're not going alone! You'll have a commanding officer, all right. In fact, you'll have the nearest thing to the perfect commanding officer in the Solar Guard!" He waited just long enough for each boy to search his mind for a suitable candidate and then added, "Your skipper will be Major Connel!"

"Major Connel!" the three cadets cried in unison.

"You mean Major 'Blast-off' Connel?" uttered Roger unbelievingly.

"That's who I mean," said Strong. "It's the best thing in the universe that could happen to you!"

Roger stood up and saluted smartly. "I request permission to be dismissed from this mission on the grounds of incompatibility, sir," he said.

"Incompatible to what?" asked Strong, amused.

"To Major Connel, sir," replied Roger.

"Permission denied," said Strong with a smile. "Buck up! It isn't so bad." Strong paused and stood up. "Well, that's it. It's close to eleven A.M. and you're to report to the major at eleven on the nose. I hope you've got the *Polaris* in good shape."

"We were up all night, sir," said Tom. "She's ready to go."

"She's in better shape than we are," said Astro.

"Very well, then. Report to Major Connel immediately. Your papers have been transferred, so all you have to do is report."

Strong rounded the desk and shook hands with each cadet. "This is an important mission, boys," he said soberly. "See that you give Major Connel all the support I know you're capable of giving. He'll need it. I doubt if I'll see you before you blast off, so this is it. Spaceman's luck to each of you!"

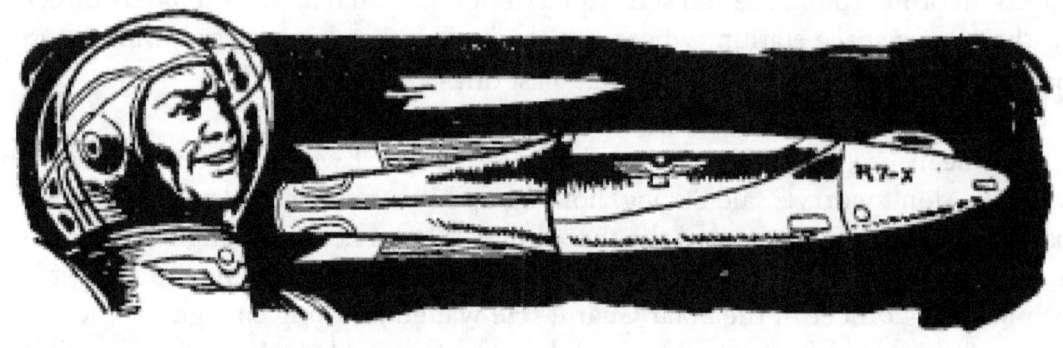

CHAPTER 3

Well, looks like we're big boys now," said Tom, as the three cadets strolled down the corridor away from Captain Strong's office. "They don't hand out secret and important missions to cadet units unless they're really on the ball!"

"But we've got Major 'Blast-off' Connel to educate," grumbled Roger.

"What do you mean 'educate'?" asked Astro.

"You know he's the roughest officer in the Academy," replied the blond-haired cadet. "He eats cadets for breakfast, lunch, and dinner. And then has an extra one for dessert. He isn't just tough—his hide's made of armor plate. But I've got a hunch that if we play dumb at first, then smarten up slowly, we can make him feel that he's done it for us. So he'll be easier on us."

"Say, it's after eleven!" exclaimed Tom. "We'd better hurry!"

Suddenly, as if a rocket cruiser were blasting off in the corridors, a roar, deafening and powerful, filled their ears. And beneath its ferocity there were four unmistakable words:

"*Polaris unit—staaaaaaaannnnnddddddd toooooo!*"

Every muscle, every bone in their three bodies snapped to rigid attention simultaneously. Eyes straight, chins in, the cadets waited for whatever calamity had befallen them. From behind came quick, heavy footsteps. They drew closer until they passed alongside and then abruptly stopped. There, in front of them, stood the one and only Major "Blast-off" Connel!

Though a few inches shorter than Astro, he was what Astro might become in thirty years, heavily muscular, with a barrel chest that filled the gold-and-black uniform tightly. He stood balanced on the balls of his small feet like a boxer, hands hanging loosely at his sides. A bulldog chin jutted out of his rough-hewn face as if it were going to snap off the head of the nearest cadet. He towered over Tom and Roger, and though shorter than Astro, he made up for this by sheer force of personality. When he spoke, his voice was like a deep foghorn that had suddenly learned the use of vowels.

"So this is the great *Polaris* unit, eh?" he bellowed. "You're two minutes late!"

Tom suddenly felt that he and his unit-mates were all alone in the corridor with the major. He glanced to one side, then the other, cautiously, and saw it was empty. And for good reason! No one wanted to be around when "Blast-off" Connel was blasting. Cadets, enlisted men, and even officers were not safe from his sudden outbursts. He drove himself so hard that he became impatient with others who were not able to match his drive. It was not because of ego but rather to get the job at hand finished. More than once he had dressed down a captain of the Solar Guard in the same tone he used on a green Earthworm. It was legend around the Academy that once, believing he was right, he had broken into the Council Chamber itself to argue his point. He won by a unanimous decision. Nothing, but nothing, had been devised or thought of that could stop "Blast-off" Connel. Every waking moment of his adult life had been spent in the pursuit of more and more knowledge about space, space travel, and life on the other planets.

Now, his wrath at fever pitch at their being tardy, he stood in front of the cadets, turning his anger on Roger first.

"Your name's Manning, isn't it?" he growled.

"Yes, sir!" replied Roger.

"Father got a medal—used to be a Solar Guard officer?"

"That's right, sir. He was killed in space."

"I know. He was a good man. *You'll* never be the man he was, if you live ten thousand years. But if you don't *try* to be a better man than he was, you won't live five minutes with me! Is that clear, Cadet Manning?"

"Very clear, sir!" gulped Roger.

Connel turned to Astro.

"And you're the home-grown atomic-rocket genius, Venusian style, eh?"

"Yes, sir," choked Astro. "I'm from Venus."

"Bucked rockets on the old chemical burners as a kid before entering the

Academy, eh?" asked Connel. There was less than an inch and a half between Astro's face and Major Connel's jaw.

"Yes, sir," answered Astro, "I was an enlisted man before coming to the Academy."

"Well, get this, you rocket buster," roared Connel. "I want a power deck that will give me what I want, when I want it, or you'll be back in the ranks again. Is that clear, Cadet Astro?"

"Yes, sir! Everything she's got, when you want it, sir."

"And I like to have a power deck clean enough to eat off the deck plates!"

"Yes, sir," stuttered Astro, growing more and more confused. "You like to eat off the deck plates, sir!"

"*By the craters of Luna, no!* I don't like to eat off the deck plates, *but I want them clean enough to eat there if I want to!*"

"Yes, sir!" Astro's voice was hardly above a whisper.

"And you're the tactical wizard that won the space maneuvers recently, single-handed, eh?" asked Connel, bending down to face Tom.

"Our side won, sir. If that answers your question," replied Tom. He was as nervous as Roger and Astro, but he fought for control. He was determined not to be bullied.

"I didn't ask you who won!" snapped Connel. "But you're the one just the same. Control-deck cadet, eh? Well, you work with me. On the control deck there's only room for one brain, one decision, one answer. And when I'm on the control deck, that decision, answer, and brain will be mine!"

"I understand perfectly, sir," said Tom tonelessly.

Connel stepped back, fists on his hips, eying the three cadets. He had heard about their difficulty in fitting personalities together when they had first arrived at Space Academy (as described in *Stand By for Mars!*). And he had heard about their triumph over the Martian desert. He was impressed with everything he had learned about them, but he knew that he had a reputation for being tough and that this reputation usually brought out the best in cadets. Early in his long and brilliant career he had learned that his life depended on the courage and ingenuity of his fellow spacemen. When he became an instructor at the Academy, he had determined that no cadet would ever be anything but the best, and that, when they blasted off in later years, they could be depended on.

He looked at the three cadets and felt a tinge of excitement that did not show on his scowling face. "Yes," he thought, "they'll make spacemen. It'll take a little time—but they're good material."

"*Now listen to this!*" he bawled. "We blast off for the Venus space station in exactly thirty minutes. Get your gear aboard the *Polaris* and stand by to raise ship." He dropped his voice and pushed out his jaw a little farther. "This will be the toughest journey you'll ever make. You'll either come back spacemen, or you'll come back nothing. I'm going to try my best to make it"—he paused and added coldly—"*nothing!* Because if you can't take it from me, then you don't belong in space! Unit *dis*-missed!"

He turned on his heel and disappeared up the slidestairs without another look at the three rigid cadets.

"Yeah—we'll educate him, all right," said Astro softly, with a wink at Tom. "Make him think he's done everything for us."

"Ah, go blast your jets!" snarled Roger after he had found his voice.

"Come on," said Tom. "Let's get the *Polaris* ready. And, fellows, I mean *ready*!"

Bill Loring and Al Mason stood near the entrance to the control tower of the Academy spaceport and watched the three cadets of the *Polaris* scramble into the giant rocket cruiser.

"Every time I think about that Connel kicking us out of space for twelve months I wanta pound his head in with a wrench!" snarled Loring.

Mason snorted. "Well, what's the use of hanging around here?" he asked. "That Connel wouldn't have us aboard the *Polaris*, even if we were cleared and had our papers. There ain't a thing we can do!"

"Don't give up so easy. There's a fortune setting up there in space—just waiting for me and you to come and take it. And no big-shot Solar Guard officer is going to keep me from getting it!"

"Yeah—yeah," grumbled Mason, "but what are you going to do about it?"

"I'll show you what I'm going to do!" said Loring. "We're heading for Venusport."

"Venusport? By the moons of Jupiter, what are we going to do there?"

"Get a free ride to Tara!"

"But how? I only got a few hundred credits and you ain't got much more. There ain't nobody going to go fifty billion miles on nothing!"

Loring's eyes followed the massive figure of Major Connel on the slidewalk as it swept across the spaceport field toward the *Polaris*. "You just buy us a coupla seats on the next rocket to Venusport and stop asking stupid questions. When we see Major 'Blast-off' Connel again, we'll be giving the orders with a paralo-ray!"

The two disgruntled spacemen turned quickly and walked to the nearest slide-walk, disappearing around a building.

Aboard the *Polaris*, Tom confronted his two unit-mates.

"Now look, fellows. After the hard time Major Connel just gave us, let's see if we can't really stay on the ball from now on."

"All right by me, Tom," Astro said, nodding his head.

"You're having space dreams, Corbett!" drawled Roger. "No matter what we do for old 'Blast-off' we'll wind up behind the eight ball."

"But if we really try," urged Tom, "if we all do our jobs, there can't be anything for him to fuss about."

"We'll make it tough for him to give us any demerits," Astro chimed in.

"Right," said Tom.

"It won't work," grumbled Roger. "You saw the way he chewed us up, and for what? I ask you—for what?"

"He was just trying to live up to his reputation, Roger," replied Tom. "But common sense will tell you that if you're on the ball you won't get demerits."

"What's the matter, hot-shot?" growled Astro. "Afraid of a little work?"

"Listen, you Venusian clunk," sneered Roger, "I'll work the pants off you any day in the week, and that includes Titan days, too!"

"O.K." Tom smiled. "Save half of that energy for the *Polaris*, Roger."

"Yeah, use some of that Manning hot air to shine brass!" suggested Astro.

"Come on. Let's get this wagon in shape," said Tom. He turned to the instrument panel and the great control board.

A moment later the three cadets were busy shining the few bits of brass and rechecking the many controls and levers. Suddenly there was the sound of a hatch slamming below and then Astro's voice came whispering over the intercom, "...

watch it, fellows. Here he comes!"

The airtight hatch leading to the control deck slid back, and Major Connel stepped inside. With one sweeping glance he took in the control deck and the evidence of their work.

"Unit— ***staaaaand to!***" he roared.

Astro climbed into the control deck and snapped to attention with his unit-mates as Connel began a quick but thorough check of the many dials and switches and relays on the control panel.

"Ummmmh," he mused. "Been doing a little work, I see."

"Oh, nothing special, sir," said Roger.

"Well, from now on it's going to be special!" roared Connel.

"Yes, sir," acknowledged Roger quickly.

"All right, at ease," ordered Connel. As the three boys relaxed, Connel stepped over to the astrogation board and snapped a switch. Immediately a solar chart filled the huge chart screen. It was a black-and-white view of the planet Venus.

"This is where we're going first," he said, placing a finger on a ball-shaped satellite in orbit around the misty planet. "This is the Venus space station. As you know, Venus has no natural satellite of its own, so we built one. We'll blast off from here and go directly to the space station where the *Polaris* will be fitted with hyperdrive for deep-space operations. While at the station you will acquaint yourselves with the operation of the new audio communications transmitter. When I'm satisfied that you can handle it under the prevailing conditions of an extended space flight, we'll blast off for a test of its range and performance."

Major Connel paused and faced the cadets squarely. Then he continued: "This is an important mission—one which I hope will enable the Solar Guard to establish the first base outside of our solar system. Our destination is Tara, in the star system of Alpha Centauri. Tara is a planet in a stage of development similar to that of Earth several million years ago. Its climate is tropical, and lush vegetation—jungles really—covers the land surface. Two great oceans separate the land masses. One is called Alpha, the other Omega. I was on the first expedition, when Tara was discovered, and have just returned from the second, during which we explored it and ran tests to learn if it could sustain human life. All tests show that Tara can be transformed into a paradise."

Connel paused, took a deep breath, and continued: "I shall expect more than just hard work from you. I want everything you have to offer. Not just good performance, but *excellence*! I will not tolerate anything less, and if I'm forced to resort to extreme disciplinary action to get what I demand, then you can expect to receive every demerit in the book!" He stepped closer to the three cadets. "Remember! Spacemen—or *nothing!* Now, stand by to blast off!"

Without a word, the three cadets hurried to their stations and began routine procedure to raise ship.

"All departments ready to blast off, Major Connel," reported Tom, saluting sharply.

"Very well, Corbett, proceed," said Connel.

Tom called into the intercom, "Stand by for blast-off!" He then opened the circuit to the teleceiver screen overhead and spoke to the spaceport control tower.

"*Polaris* to spaceport control. Request permission to blast off. Request orbit."

"Spaceport traffic to *Polaris*. Your orbit has been cleared 089—repeat 089—blast off in two minutes ..."

"Orbit 089—blast off minus one fifty-nine fifty-eight."

"You read me clear, *Polaris* ..."

Tom clicked off the switch and turned to the intercom. "Control deck to radar bridge. Do we have a clear tangent forward and up?"

"All clear forward and up, Tom," replied Roger.

"Control deck to power deck. Energize the cooling pumps!"

"Cooling pumps in operation," answered Astro briskly.

The giant ship began to shudder as the mighty pumps on the power deck started their slow, whining build-up. Tom sat in front of the control panel, strapped himself into the acceleration chair, and began checking the dials and gauges. Satisfied everything was in order, he fastened his eyes to the sweeping red second hand on the solar clock. The teleceiver screen brought a sharp picture of the surrounding base of the spaceship, and he saw that it was all clear. The second hand reached the ten-second mark.

"Stand by to raise ship!" bawled Tom into the intercom. The red hand moved steadily, surely, to the zero at the top of the clock face. Tom reached for the master switch.

"Blast off minus five—four—three—two—one—*zero!*"

Tom threw the switch.

Slowly the giant ship raised itself from the ground. Then faster and faster, pushing the four spacemen deep into their acceleration cushions, it hurtled spaceward.

In a few seconds the *Polaris* was gravity-free. Once again, Earthmen had started another journey to the stars.

CHAPTER 4

Stand by to reduce speed three-quarters!" roared Major Connel.

"Aye, aye, sir," replied Tom, and began the necessary adjustments on the control panel. He spoke into the intercom. "Control deck to power deck. Stand by to reduce thrust on main drive rockets by three-quarters. We're coming onto the space station, Astro."

"Power deck, aye," acknowledged Astro.

Drifting in a steady orbit around its mother planet, the Venus space station loomed ahead of the *Polaris* like a huge metal ball set against a backdrop of cold, black space. It was studded with gaping holes, air locks which served as landing ports for spaceships. Inside the station was a compact city. Living quarters, communications rooms, repair shops, weather observations, meteor information, everything to serve the great fleet of Solar Guard and merchant spaceships plying the space lanes between Earth, Mars, Venus, and Titan.

"I'm getting the identification request from the station, sir. Shall I answer her?" asked Roger over the intercom.

"Of course, you space-brained idiot, and make it fast!" exploded Connel. "What do you want to do? Get us blasted out of space?"

"Yes, sir!" replied Roger. "Right away, sir!"

Tom kept his eyes on the teleceiver screen above his head. The image of the space station loomed large and clear.

"Approaching a little too fast, I think, sir," volunteered Tom. "Shall I make the adjustment?"

"What's the range?" asked Connel.

Tom named a figure.

"Ummmmh," mused Connel. He glanced quickly over the dials and then nodded in assent. Tom turned once more to the intercom. "Control deck to power deck," he called. "Stand by for maneuvering, Astro, and reduce your main drive thrust to minimum space speed."

"Space station traffic control to rocket cruiser *Polaris*. Come in, *Polaris*. This is traffic control on space station to *Polaris*," the audio teleceiver crackled.

"Rocket cruiser *Polaris* to space station and traffic control. Request touch-down permission and landing-port number," replied Tom.

"Permission to touch down granted, *Polaris*. You are to line up on approach to landing-port seven—repeat—seven. Am now sending out guiding radar beam. Can you read beam?"

Tom turned to the intercom. "Have you got the station's guiding beam, Roger?"

"All lined up, Tom," replied Roger from the radar bridge. "Get that Venusian on the power deck to give me a three-second shot on the starboard rocket, if he can find the right handles!"

"I heard that, Manning!" roared Astro's voice on the intercom. "Another crack like that and I'll make you get out and push this baby around!"

"*You execute that order and do it blasted quick!*" Major Connel's voice exploded over the intercom. "And watch that loose talk on the ship's intercom. From now on, all directions and orders will be given and received in a crisp, clear manner without unnecessary familiarity!"

Connel didn't expect them to acknowledge his order. The cadets had heard him and that was enough. He knew it was enough. In the short time it had taken them to traverse the immense gulf of space between the Academy and the station Connel had handed out demerits by fives and tens! Each of the cadets was now tagged with enough black marks to spend two months in the galley working them off!

Now, working together like the smooth team of junior spacemen they were, Tom, Roger, and Astro maneuvered the great rocket ship toward the gaping hole of the air lock in the side of the white ball-like satellite.

"Drop your bow one half degree, *Polaris*, you're up too high," warned the station control.

"A short burst on the upper trim rocket, Astro," called Tom.

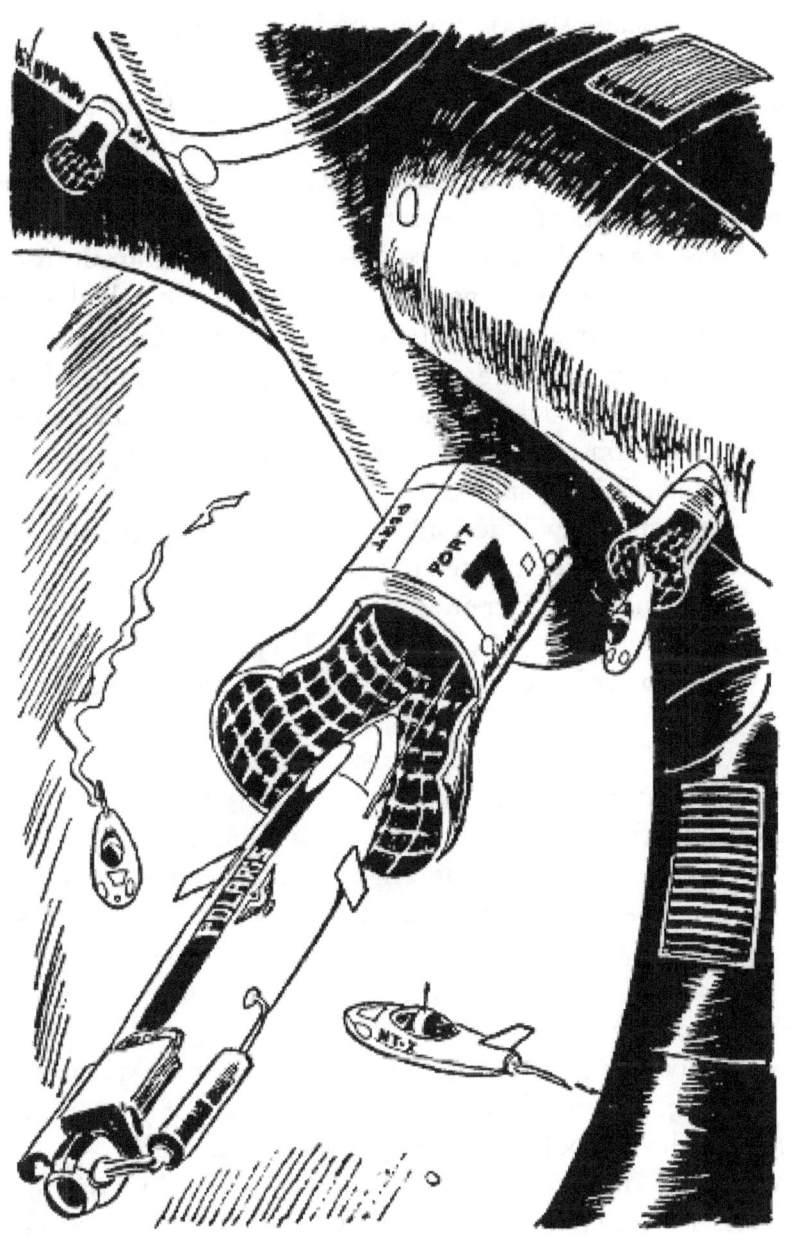

The junior spaceman maneuvered the great rocket ship toward the air lock

The great ship bucked slightly under the force of sudden thrust, and then its nose dropped the required half degree.

"Cut all thrust and brake your speed to dead ship, *Polaris*," ordered traffic control.

Again Tom relayed the order to Astro, and a moment later the great ship hung silently in the airless void of space, a scant half mile from the station.

Through the teleceiver Tom could see the jet boats darting out from the station carrying the magnetic cables. In a moment the lines were attached to the steel skin of the ship, and gradually the lines tightened, pulling the mighty spaceship into the waiting port. Once inside, the outer air lock was closed and the *Polaris* was slung in the powerful magnetic cradles that held her in a rigid position. Elsewhere on the satellite, quick calculations were made for the additional weight, and the station was counterbalanced to assure an even orbit around Venus.

Tom flicked the many switches off on the great board, glanced at the time of arrival on the solar clock, and reported to Major Connel.

"Touchdown at one-nine-four-nine, sir."

"Very well, Corbett," answered Connel. Then he added grudgingly, "That was as fine a job of control-deck operations as I've seen. Keep up the good work, spaceman."

Tom gulped. The unexpected compliment caught him off guard. And he was even more pleased that for the first time Connel had referred to him as spaceman!

"I'll be needed at the space station commander's quarters for a while, Corbett," said Connel. "Meanwhile, you and Manning and Astro acquaint yourselves with the station. Report to me back aboard the ship in exactly two hours. Dismissed."

Tom saluted, and Connel disappeared toward the exit port.

"Well, *spaceman*," Roger drawled casually from behind, "it looks like you've got yourself in solid with the old man!"

Tom smiled. "With a guy like that, Roger, you're never in solid. Maybe I did get a pat on the back, but you didn't hear him cancel any of those demerits he gave me for not signing the logbook after that last watch, did you?"

"Let's get some chow," growled Astro, who came hustling through the hatch. "I'm half starved. By the craters of Luna, how many times can you change course in five minutes?"

Astro referred to the countless times Tom had had to call for fraction-degree course changes in their approach to the gaping entrance port.

Tom laughed. "With Connel on the bridge, you're lucky I didn't give you twice as many," he replied. "Can you imagine what would have happened if we had missed and hit the station?"

"Brrrrrr!" shuddered Roger. "I hate to think about it. Come on. Let's rustle up some grub for the Venusian. I could use some myself."

The three boys quickly changed to their dress blue cadet uniforms and left the ship. A moment later they were being whisked up an electric elevator to the main—or "street"—level. The door opened, and they stepped out into a large circular area about the size of a city block in the rear of the station. The area had been broken into smaller sections. One side of the "street" was devoted to shops, a small stereo house which was playing the latest Liddy Tamal hit, "Children of Space" (a sensational drama about the lives of men in the future), restaurants, and even a curio shop. The Venus space station handled ninety per cent of the traffic into and out of Venusport. It was a refueling stop for the jet liners and space freighters bound for the outer planets, and for those returning to Earth. Some ships went directly to Venusport for heavy overhaul or supplies, but the station was established primarily for quick turn arounds. Several ex-enlisted spacemen who had been injured or retired were given special permission to open shops for the convenience of the passengers and crews of the ships and the staff of the station. In twenty years the station had become a place where summer tourists from Earth and winter tourists from Titan made a point of stopping. The first of its kind in the universe, it was as near a perfect place to live as could be built by man.

Tom, Roger, and Astro strolled down the short street, pushing through a crowd of tourists admiring the shops. Finally they found a restaurant that specialized in Venusian dishes.

"Now you two spindly Earthmen are going to have the best meal of your lives! Broiled dinosaur on real Venusian black bread!"

"D-dinosaur!" stuttered Tom in amazement. "Why—why—that's a prehistoric monster!"

"Yeah, Astro," agreed Roger. "What are you trying to hand us?"

Astro laughed. "You'll see, fellows," he replied. "I used to go hunting for them when I was a kid. Brought the best price of any wild game. Fifty credits for babies under three hundred pounds. Over that, you can't eat 'em. Too tough!"

Tom and Roger looked at each other, eyes bulging.

"Ah, come on, Tom," drawled Roger. "He's just trying to pull our leg."

Without a word, Astro grabbed them by the arms and rushed them into the restaurant. They were no sooner seated when a recorded voice announced the menu over a small loud-speaker on the table. Astro promptly ordered dinosaur, and to his unit-mates' amazement, the voice politely inquired:

"Would the spacemen prefer to have it broiled a la Venusian black bread, baked, or raw?"

A sharp look from Roger and Tom, and Astro ordered it broiled.

One hour and fifteen minutes later the three members of the *Polaris* unit staggered out of the restaurant.

"By the rings of Saturn," declared Tom, "that wasn't only the most I ever ate—it was the best!"

Roger nodded in silent agreement, leaning against the plastic window in front of the restaurant.

"You see," Astro beamed, "maybe you guys will listen to me from now on!"

"Boy, I can't wait to see Mom's face when I tell her that her chicken and dumplings have taken second place to broiled monster!"

"By the jumping blazes of the stars!" yelled Roger suddenly. "Look at the time! We're ten minutes late!"

"Ohhhhh," moaned Tom. "I knew it was too good to be true!"

"Step on it!" said Astro. "Maybe he won't notice."

"Some chance," groaned Roger, running after Tom and Astro. "That old rocket head wouldn't miss anything!"

The three boys raced back to the electric elevator and were silently whisked to the air-lock level. They hurried aboard the *Polaris* and into the control room. Major Connel was seated in a chair near the chart screen, studying some papers. The cadets drew themselves to attention.

"Unit reporting for duty, sir," Tom quavered.

Connel spun around in the swivel chair, glanced at the clock, put the papers to one side, and slowly advanced toward the cadets.

"Thirteen and a half minutes late!" he said, dropping his voice to a biting growl. "I'll give you five seconds to think up a good excuse. Every man is entitled to an excuse. Some have good ones, some have truthful ones, and some have excuses that sound as though they made them up in five seconds!"

He eyed the cadets speculatively. "Well?" he demanded.

"I'm afraid we were carried away by our enthusiasm for a meal Astro introduced us to, sir," said Tom honestly.

"All right," snapped Connel, "then here's something else to carry you all away!" He paused and rocked on the balls of his feet. "I had planned to give you three liberty of the station while here, whenever you weren't working on the new transmitter. But since you have shown yourselves to be carried away so easily, I don't think I can depend on your completing your regular duties. Therefore, I suggest that each of you report to the officer in charge of your respective departments and learn the operation and function of the station while we're here. This work will be *in addition* to your assigned duties on the new transmitter operation!"

The three cadets gulped but were silent.

"Not only that," Connel's voice had risen to an angry bark, "but you will be logged a demerit apiece for each minute you reported late. Thirteen and a half minutes, thirteen and a half demerits!"

The gold and black of the Solar Guard uniform never looked more ominous as the three cadets watched the stern spaceman turn and stomp out the exit port.

Alone, their liberty taken away from them before they even knew they had it, the boys sat around on the control deck of the silent ship and listened to the distant throb of a pump, rising and falling, pumping free air throughout the station.

"Well," sighed Tom, "I always did want to know how a space station worked. Now I guess I'll learn firsthand."

"Me, too," said Astro. He propped his big feet up on a delicate instrument panel of the control board.

"Me, too!" sneered Roger, his voice filled with a bitterness that surprised Tom and Astro. "But I didn't think I would find out like this! How in the universe has that—that tyrant managed to stay alive this long!"

CHAPTER 5

The space station's biggest headache," said Terry Scott, a young Solar Guard officer assigned the job of showing the *Polaris* crew around, "is to maintain perfect balance at all times."

"How do you achieve that, sir?" asked Tom.

"We create our own gravity by means of a giant gyroscope in the heart of the station. When more weight is taken aboard, or weight leaves the station, we have to adjust the gyro's speed."

They entered the power deck of the great ball-like satellite. Astro's eyes glowed with pleasure as he glanced approvingly from one massive machine to another. The fuel tanks were made of thin durable aluminite; a huge cylinder, covered with heat-resistant paint, was the air conditioner; power came from a bank of atomic dynamos and generators; while those massive pumps kept the station's artificial air and water supply circulating.

Dials, gauges, meters, were arrayed in seemingly endless rows—but each one of them actually played its part in keeping the station in balance.

Astro's face was one big, delighted grin.

"Well," said Roger with a sly wink at Tom, "you can't tell me that Connel has made our Venusian unhappy. Even if he had given us liberty, I'll bet Astro would have spent it down here with the grease monkeys!"

Astro didn't rise to the bait. His attention was riveted on a huge dynamo, which he watched with appreciative eyes. But then Terry Scott introduced the *Polaris* unit to an older Solar Guard officer.

"Cadets, meet Captain Jenledge," said Scott. "And, sir, this is Cadet Astro. Major Connel would like him to work with you while he's here."

"Glad to know you, boys," said Jenledge, "and particularly you, Cadet Astro.

I've heard about your handiness with the thrust buckets on the cruisers. What do you think of our layout?"

The officer turned and waved his hand to indicate the power-deck equipment.

"This is just about the finest—the most terrif—"

The officer smiled at Astro's inability to describe his feelings. Jenledge was proud of his power deck, proud of the whole establishment, for that matter. He had conceived it, had drawn the plans, and had constructed this space station.

Throughout the solar system it was considered his baby. And when he had asked for permission to remain on as senior power-deck chief, the Solar Alliance had jumped at the chance to keep such a good man on the job. The station had become a sort of postgraduate course for power-deck cadets and junior Solar Guard officers.

Astro beamed. So, the great Jenledge had actually heard of him—of humble Cadet Astro. He could hardly restrain himself from ripping off his blue uniform and going right to work on a near-by machine that had been torn apart for repairs. Finally he managed to gasp, "I think it's great, sir—just wonderful!"

"Very well, Cadet Astro," said the officer. "There's a pair of coveralls in my locker. You can start right to work." He paused and his eyes twinkled. "If you want to, that is!"

"Want to!" roared Astro, and was off to the locker room.

Jenledge turned to Scott. "Leave him with me, Scotty. I don't think Cadet Astro's going to care much about the rest of the station!"

Scott smiled, saluted, and walked away. Tom and Roger came to attention, saluted, and followed the young officer off the power deck.

"Astro's probably happier now than he'll ever be in his life, Tom," whispered Roger.

"Yeah," agreed Tom. "Did you see the way his eyes lit up when we walked in there? Like a kid with a brand-new toy!"

A moment later Scott, Tom, and Roger, in a vacuum elevator, were being hurtled to the station's upper decks. They got out on the observation deck, and Scott walked directly to a small door at the end of a corridor. A light over the door flashed red and Scott stopped.

"Here's the weather and meteor observation room," he said. "Also radar communications. When the red light's on, it means photographs are being taken. We'll have to wait for them to finish."

As they waited, Tom and Roger talked to Scott. He had graduated from Space Academy seven years before, they learned. He'd been assigned to the Solar Alliance Chamber as liaison between the Chamber and the Solar Guard. After four years, he had requested a transfer to active space operations.

Then, he told them, there'd been an accident. His ship exploded. He'd been badly injured—in fact, both his legs were now artificial.

The cadets, who had thought him a bit stuffy at first, were changing their minds fast. Why hadn't he quit, they wanted to know?

"Leave space?" said Scott. "I'd rather die. I can't blast off any more. But here at the station I'm still a spaceman."

The red light went out, and they opened the door.

In sharp contrast to the bustle and noise on the power deck, the meteor, weather, and radar observation room was filled with only a subdued whisper. All around them huge screens displayed various views of the surface of Venus as it slowly revolved beneath the station. Along one side of the room was a solid bank of four-foot-square teleceiver screens with an enlisted spaceman or junior officer seated in front of each one. These men, at their microphones, were relaying meteor and weather information to all parts of the solar system. Now it was Roger's turn to get excited at seeing the wonderful radar scanners that swept space for hundreds of thousands of miles. They were powerful enough to pick up a spaceship's identifying outline while still two hundred thousand miles away! Farther to one side, a single teleceiver screen, ten feet square, dominated the room. Roger gasped.

Scott smiled. "That's the largest teleceiver screen in the universe," he said. "The most powerful. And it's showing you a picture of the Andromeda Galaxy, thousands of light years away. Most of the lights you see there are no more than that, just light, their stars, or suns, having long ago exploded or burned. But the light continues to travel, taking thousands of years to reach our solar system."

"But—but—" gasped Tom. "How can you be so accurate with this screen? It looks as though we were smack in the center of the galaxy itself!"

"There's a fifty-inch telescope attached to the screen," Scott replied, "which is equal to the big one-thousand-inch 'eye' back at the Academy."

"Why is that, sir?" asked Roger.

"You don't get any distortion from atmosphere up here," replied the young officer.

As Tom and Roger walked silently among the men at the teleceiver screens, Scott continued to explain. "This is where you'll be, Manning," he said, indicating a large radarscope scanner a little to one side and partially hidden from the glow of the huge teleceiver screen. "We need a man on watch here twenty-four hours a day, though there isn't much doing between midnight and eight A.M. on radar watch. A little traffic, but nothing compared to what we get during the regular working day."

"Any particular reason for that, sir?" asked Tom.

"Oh, there just aren't many arrivals and departures during that period. We have night crews to handle light traffic, but by midnight the station is pretty much like any sleepy Middle Western town. Rolls up the sidewalks and goes to bed."

He motioned to Roger to follow him to the radar section and left Tom watching the interesting spectacle on the giant televeiver. A huge star cluster flashed brilliantly, filling the screen with light, then faded into the endless blackness of space. Tom caught his breath as he remembered what Scott had told him about the light being thousands of years old before reaching the solar system.

"Manning's all set, Corbett," said Scott at Tom's elbow. "Come on. I'll show you the traffic-control deck."

Tom followed the young officer out of the room. As all true spacemen do at one time or another in their lives, he thought about the pitifully small part mankind had played so far in the conquest of the stars. Man had come a long way, Tom was ready to admit, but there was still a lot of work ahead for young, courageous spacemen.

As Scott and Tom climbed the narrow stairs to the traffic-control deck, the Solar Guard officer continued to speak of the man-made satellite. "When the station was first built," he said, "it was expected to be just a way station for refueling and celestial observations. But now we're finding other uses for it, just as though it were a small community on Earth, Mars, or Venus. In fact, they're now planning to build still larger stations." Scott opened the door to the traffic-control room. He motioned to Tom to follow him.

This room, Tom was ready to admit, was the busiest place he had ever seen in his life. All around the circular room enlisted Solar Guardsmen sat at small desks, each with a monitoring board in front of him holding three televeiver screens. As he talked into a mike near by, each man, by shifting from one screen to the next, was able to follow the progress of a spaceship into or out of the landing ports. One thing puzzled Tom. He turned to Scott.

"Sir, how come some of those screens show the *station* from the *outside*?" he asked. Tom pointed to a screen in front of him that had a picture of a huge jet liner just entering a landing port.

"Two-way televeivers, Corbett," said Scott with a smile. "When you arrived on the *Polaris*, didn't you have a view of the station on your televeiver?"

"Yes, sir," answered Tom, "of course."

"Well, these monitors picked up your image on the *Polaris* televeiver. So the traffic-control chief here could see exactly what you were seeing."

In the center of the circular room Tom noticed a round desk that was raised about eight feet from the floor. This desk dominated all activity in the busy room. Inside it stood a Solar Guard officer, watching the monitoring teleceivers. He wore a throat microphone for sending out messages, and for receiving calls had a thin silver wire running to the vibrating bone in his ear. He moved constantly, turning in a circle, watching the various landing ports on the many screens. Three-thousand-ton rocket liners, Solar Guard cruisers, scout ships, and destroyers all moved about the satellite lazily, waiting for permission to enter or depart. This man was the master traffic-control officer who had first contacted Tom on his approach to the station. He did that for all approaching ships—contacted them, got the recognition signal, found out the ship's destination, its weight, and its cargo or passenger load.

Then the connection was relayed to one of the secondary control officers at the monitoring boards.

"That's Captain Stefens," said Scott in a whisper. "Toughest officer on the station. He has to be. From five hundred to a thousand ships arrive and depart daily. It's his job to see that every arriving ship is properly taken into the landing ports. Besides that, everything you've seen, except the meteor and weather observation rooms, are under his command. If he thinks a ship is overloaded, he won't allow it to enter and disrupt the balance of the station. Instead, he'll order its skipper to dump part of his cargo out in space to be picked up later. He makes hundreds of decisions a day—some of them really hair-raising. Once, when a rocket scout crew was threatened with exploding reactant mass, he calmly told them to blast off into a desolate spot in space and blow up. The crew could have abandoned ship, but they chose to remain with it and were blown to atoms. It could have happened to the station. That night he got a three-day pass from the station and went to Venusport."

Scott shook his head. "I've heard Venusport will never be the same after that three-day pass of Captain Stefens."

The young officer looked at Corbett quizzically. "That's the man you're going to work for."

Scott walked over to the circular desk and spoke rapidly to the officer inside. As Tom approached, Stefens gave him a quick, sharp glance. It sent a shiver down the cadet's spine. Scott waved to him to come over.

"Captain Stefens, this is Cadet Tom Corbett."

Tom came to attention.

"All right, Corbett," said Stefens, speaking like a man who had a lot to do, knew how to do it, liked to do it, and was losing time. "Stand up here with me and keep your mouth shut. Remember any questions you want to ask, and when I have a spare moment, ask them. And by the rings of Saturn, be sure I'm free to answer. Take my attention at the wrong moment and we could have a bad accident."

Stefens gave Scott a fleeting smile and turned back to his constant keen-eyed inspection of the monitors.

The radar watch was reporting the approach of a ship. Stefens began his cold, precise orders.

"Monitor seven, take freighter out of station on port sixty-six; monitor twelve, stand by for identification signal of jet liner coming in from Mars. Watch her closely. The Venusport Space Line is overloading again...." On and on he went, with Tom standing to one side watching with wide-eyed wonder as the many ships were maneuvered into and out of the station.

Suddenly Stefens turned to Tom. "Well, Corbett," he rasped, "what's the first question?"

Tom gulped. He had been so fascinated by the room's sheer magic and by Stefens' sure control of the traffic that he hadn't had a chance to think.

"I—I—don't have one—yet, sir," he managed finally.

"I want five questions within five minutes!" snapped Stefens, "and they better be rocket-blasting *good questions*!" He turned back to the monitors.

Tom Corbett, while he had gained the respect of many elder spacemen, was discovering that a cadet's life got no easier as time went on. He wondered fleetingly how Roger and Astro were making out, and then he began to think of some questions.

Beside him, oblivious of his presence, Stefens continued to spout directions. "Monitor three, take rocket scout out of landing-port eight. One crew member is remaining aboard the station for medical treatment. He weighs one hundred and fifty-eight pounds. Make balance adjustments accordingly...."

Tom's head was spinning. It was all too much for one young cadet to absorb on such short notice.

CHAPTER 6

There goes the jet liner to Mars," said Al Mason wistfully. "Sure wish we wuz on her." His eyes followed the beautiful slim passenger ship just blasting off from Venus.

"Why?" demanded Loring.

"Anything to get away from Venusport. What a stinking hole!" snorted the shorter of the two spacemen.

"For what we want to do," said Loring, "there ain't another city in the system that's got the advantages this place has!"

"Don't talk to me about advantages," whined Mason. "Be darned if I can see any. All we been doing is hang around the spaceport, talk to the spacemen, and watch the ships blast off. Maybe you're up to something but I'm blasted if I see what it can be."

"I've been looking for the right break to come along."

"What kind of break?" growled Mason.

"That kind," said Loring. He pointed to a distant figure emerging from a space freighter. "There's our answer!" said Loring, a note of triumph in his voice. "Come on. Let's get outta here. I don't want to be recognized."

"But—but—what's up? What's that guy and the space freighter *Annie Jones* got to do with us?"

Loring didn't answer but stepped quickly to the nearest jet cab and hopped into the back seat. Mason tumbled in after him.

"Spaceman's Row," Loring directed, "and make it quick!"

The driver stepped on the accelerator and the red teardrop-shaped vehicle shot away from the curb into the crowd of cars racing along Premier Highway Number One.

The jet cab raced along the highway to Venusport

In the back seat of the jet cab, Loring turned to his spacemate and slapped him on the back.

"Soon's we get into the Row, you go and pack our gear, see! Then meet me at the Cafe Cosmos in half an hour."

"Pack our gear?" asked Mason with alarm. "Are we going some place?"

Loring shot a glance at the driver. "Just do as I tell you!" he growled. "In a few hours we'll be on our way to Tara, and then—" He dropped his voice to a whisper. Mason listened and smiled.

The jet cab slid along the arrow-straight highway toward the heart of the city of Venusport. Soon it reached the outskirts. On both sides of the highway rose low, flat-roofed dwellings, built on a revolving wheel to follow the precious sun, and constructed of pure Titan crystal. Farther ahead and looming magnificent in the late afternoon sun was the first and largest of Venusian cities, Venusport. Like a fantastically large diamond, the startling towers of the young city shot upward into the misty atmosphere, catching the light and reflecting it in every color of the spectrum.

Loring and Mason did not appreciate the beauty of the city as they rode swiftly through the busy streets. Loring, in particular, thought as he had never thought before. He was busily putting a plot together in his mind—a plot as dangerous as it was criminal.

The jet cab slammed to a stop at a busy intersection of the city. This was Spaceman's Row, and it dated back to Venusport's first rough and tough pioneering days.

For two blocks on either side of the street, in building after building, cafes, pawnshops, cheap restaurants above and below the street level, supplied the needs of countless shadowy figures who came and went as silently as ghosts. Spaceman's Row was where suspended spacemen and space rats, prospectors of the asteroids for uranium and pitchblende, gathered and found short-lived and rowdy fun. Here, skippers of rocket ships, bound for destinations in deep space, could find hands willing to sign on their dirty freighters despite low pay and poor working conditions. No questions were asked here. Along Spaceman's Row, hard men played a grim game of survival.

Loring and Mason paid the driver, got out, and walked down the busy street.

Here and there, nuaniam signs began to flick on, their garish blues, reds, and whites bathing the street in a glow of synthetic light. It was early evening, but already Spaceman's Row was getting ready for the coming night.

Presently, Mason left Loring, climbing up a long narrow flight of stairs leading to a dingy back hall bedroom to pack their few remaining bits of gear.

Loring walked on amid the noise and laughter that echoed from cheap restaurants and saloons. Stopping before Cafe Cosmos, he surveyed the street quickly before entering the wide doors. Many years before, the Cosmos had been a sedate dining spot, a place where respectable family parties came to enjoy good food and the gentle breezes of a near-by lake. Now, with the lake polluted by industry and with the gradual influx of shiftless spacemen, the Cosmos had been given over to the most basic, simple need of its new patrons—rocket juice!

The large room that Loring entered still retained some of the features of its more genteel beginnings, but the huge blaring teleceiver screen was filled with the pouting face of a popular singer. He advanced to the bar that occupied one entire wall.

"Rocket juice!" he said, slamming down his fist on the wooden bar. "Double!" He was served a glass of the harsh bluish liquid, paid his credits, and downed the drink. Then he turned slowly and glanced around the half-filled room. Almost immediately he spotted a small wizened man limping toward him.

"Been waiting for you," said the man.

"Well," demanded Loring, "did'ja get anything set up, Shinny?"

"*Mr.* Shinny!" growled the little man, with surprising vigor. "I'm old enough to be your father!"

"Awright—awright—*Mr.* Shinny!" sneered Loring. "Did'ja get it?"

The little man shook his head. "Nothing on the market, Billy boy." He paused and aimed a stream of tobacco juice at a near-by cuspidor.

Loring looked relieved. "Just as well. I've got something else lined up, anyway."

Shinny's eyes sharpened. "You must have a pretty big strike, Billy boy, if you're so hot to buy a spaceship!"

"Only want to take a little ride upstairs, *Mr.* Shinny," said Loring.

"Don't hand me that space gas!" snapped Shinny. "A man who's lost his space papers ain't going to take a chance at getting caught by the Solar Guard, busting the void with a rocket ship and no papers." He stopped, and his small gray eyes twinkled. "*Unless*," he added, "you've got quite a strike lined up!"

"Hey, Loring!" yelled Mason, entering the cafe. He carried two spaceman's traveling bags, small black plastic containers with glass zippers.

"So you've got Al Mason in with you," mused Shinny. "Pretty good man, Al. Let's see now, I saw you two just before you blasted off for Tara!" He paused. "Couldn't be that you've got anything lined up in deep space, now could it?"

"You're an old fool!" snarled Loring.

"Heh—heh—heh," chuckled Shinny. A toothless smile spread across his wrinkled face. "Coming close, am I?"

Al Mason looked at Shinny and back at Loring. "Say! What is this?" he demanded.

"O.K., O.K.," said Loring between clenched teeth. "So we've got a strike out in the deep, but one word outta line from you and I'll blast you with my heater!"

"Not a word," said Shinny, "not a word. I'll only charge you a little to keep your secret."

Mason looked at Loring. "How much?" he demanded.

"A twentieth of the take," said Shinny. "And that's dirt cheap."

"It's robbery," said Loring, "but O.K. We've got no choice!"

"Loring, wait a minute!" objected Mason. "One twentieth! Why, that could add up to a million credits!"

Shinny's eyes opened wide. "Twenty million! Hey, there hasn't been a uranium strike that big since the old seventeenth moon of Jupiter back in 2294!"

Loring motioned to them to sit down at a table. He ordered a bottle of rocket juice and filled three glasses.

"This ain't uranium, *Mr.* Shinny!" he said.

Shinny's eyes opened wider still. "What then?"

"What's the most precious metal in the system today?" Loring asked.

"Why—gold, I guess."

"Next to gold?"

Shinny thought for a moment. "Couldn't be silver any more, since they're making the artificial stuff cheaper'n it costs to mine it." The little man's jaw dropped and he stared at Loring. "You mean—?"

"That's right," said Loring, "copper!"

Shinny's mind raced. In this year of 2353, all major copper deposits had long since been exhausted and only small new deposits were being found, not nearly enough for the needs of the expanding system. In an age of electronics, lack of copper had become a serious bottleneck in the production of electrical and scientific equipment. Search parties were out constantly, all over the solar system, trying to find more of the precious stuff. So a deposit of the kind Loring and Mason were talking about was a prize indeed.

Shinny's greedy fingers twitched with anticipation.

"So that's why you want to buy a spaceship, eh?"

"Wanted," replied Loring. "I don't want to buy one now. The way things look, we'll get what we want for nothing!"

Mason, who had been sitting quietly, suddenly jumped up. "So that's your angle! Well, I don't want any part of it," he shouted.

Loring and Shinny looked up in surprise.

"What're you talking about?" demanded Loring.

"All of a sudden it's come to me. Now I know why you've been hanging around the spaceport for the last two weeks. And what you meant when you saw the spaceman get out of that freighter today!"

"Sit down!" barked Loring. "If you weren't so dumb, you'd have caught on long ago." He eyed the shorter man from between half-closed lids. "It's the only way we can get out of here!"

"Not me. I ain't pulling anything like that!" whined Mason.

"What's going on here?" demanded Shinny. "What're you two space bums talking about?"

"I'll tell you what! He's going to try—"

Loring suddenly stood up and slapped the shorter spaceman across the mouth. Mason sat down, a dazed look on his face.

"You space-crawling rat!" hissed Loring. "You'll do what I tell you to do, see?"

"Yeah—yeah, sure," bleated Mason. "O.K. Anything you say. Anything."

"What is this?" demanded Shinny.

"You shut up!" growled Loring.

"I won't!" said Shinny, as he also rose from the table. "You may be tough, Billy Loring, but not as tough as me!"

The two men stared at each other for a moment. Finally Loring smiled and patted Mason's shoulder. "Sorry, Al. I guess I got a little hot for a moment."

"Quit talking riddles," pleaded Shinny. "What's this all about?"

"Sit down," said Loring.

They sank back into their chairs.

"It's simple," said Mason fearfully. "Loring wants to steal a spaceship."

"A pirate job!" said Shinny. He drew in his breath sharply. "You must be outta your mind!"

"You've called yourself in on this," Loring reminded him. "And you're staying in."

"Oh, no!" Shinny's voice dropped to a husky, frightened whisper. "Deal's off. I ain't gonna spend the rest of my life on a prison asteroid!"

"Shinny, you know too much!" Loring's hand darted toward the blaster he wore at his belt.

"Your secret's safe with me. I give you my spaceman's word on it," said Shinny, pushing back his chair. Abruptly getting to his feet, he scrambled rapidly out the door of the Cafe Cosmos.

"Loring," said Mason, "get him. You can't let him ..."

"Forget it," shot back the other. "He won't break his spaceman's oath. Not Shinny." He got up. "Come on, Mason. We haven't got much time before the *Annie Jones* blasts off."

"What are we gonna do?" the shorter man wanted to know.

"Stow away on the cargo deck. Then, when we get out into space, we dump the pilots and head for Tara, for our first load of copper."

"But a job like this'll take money!"

"We'll make enough to go ahead on the first load."

Mason began to get up, hesitated, and then sat down again.

"Come on," snapped Loring. His hand dropped toward his belt. "I'm going to make you rich, Mason," he said quietly. "I'm going to make you one of the richest men in the universe—even if I have to kill you first."

CHAPTER 7

Space freighter ***Antares*** from Venus space station. Your approach course is one-nine-seven—corrected. Reduce speed to minimum thrust and approach spaceport nine—landing-deck three. End transmission!"

Tom stood on the dais of the traffic-control room and switched the ***Antares*** beam to one of his assistants at the monitors in the control room. In less than two weeks he had mastered the difficult traffic-control procedure to the point where Captain Stefens had allowed him to handle the midnight shift. He checked the monitors and turned to see Roger walk through the door.

"Working hard, Junior?" asked Roger in his casual drawl.

"Roger!" exclaimed Tom. "What are you fooling around down here for?"

"Ah, there's nothing to do on the radar deck. Besides, I've got the emergency alarm on." He wiped his forehead. "Brother! Of all the crummy places to be stuck!"

"Could be worse," said Tom, his eyes sweeping the monitors.

"Nothing could be worse," groaned Roger. "But nothing. Think of that lovely space doll Helen Ashton alone on earth—and me stuck here on a space station."

"Well, we're doing an important job, Roger," replied Tom. "And doing it well, or Major Connel wouldn't leave us alone so much. How're you making out with the new equipment?"

"That toy?" sneered Roger. "I gave it a look, checked the circuits once, and knew it inside out. It's so simple a child could have built one!"

"Oh, sure," scoffed Tom. "That's why the top scientists worked for years on something small, compact, powerful enough to reach through deep space—and still be easy to repair."

"Quit heckling me, Junior," retorted Roger, "I'm thinking. Trying to figure out some way of getting to the teleceiver set on board the *Polaris*."

"Why can't you get on the *Polaris*?" asked Tom.

"They're jazzing up the power deck with a new hyperdrive unit for the big hop to Tara. So many guys buzzing around you can't get near it."

"What do you need a teleceiver for?" asked Tom.

"To give me company," replied Roger sourly. "Say!" He snapped his fingers suddenly. "Maybe if I just changed the frequency—"

"What frequency? What are you talking about?"

"Spaceboy, I'm getting a real hot-rocket idea! See ya later!" And the blond cadet ran for the door.

Tom watched his unit-mate disappear and shook his head in amused despair. Roger, he told himself, might be difficult, but he was certainly never dull.

Then his attention was brought back to the monitors by the warning of another approaching spaceship.

"... jet liner *San Francisco* to Venus space-station traffic control ..." the metallic voice crackled over the speaker.

"Jet liner *San Francisco*, this is Venus space-station traffic control," replied Tom. "You are cleared for landing at port eleven—repeat—eleven. Make standard check for approach orbit to station landing. End transmission!"

From one side of the circular dais, Tom saw Major Connel enter the room. He snapped to attention and saluted smartly.

"Morning, Corbett," said Connel, returning Tom's salute. "Getting into the swing of the operation?"

"Yes, sir," said Tom. "I've handled about twenty approaches since Captain Stefens left me alone, and about fifty departures." Tom brought his fist up, with the thumb extended and wiped it across his chest in the traditional spaceman's signal that all was clear. "I didn't scratch one of 'em, sir," he said, smiling.

"Good enough," said Connel. "Keep it that way." He watched the monitor screen as the liner *San Francisco* settled into landing-port eleven.

When she was cradled and secure, he grunted his satisfaction and turned to leave. At the door he suddenly paused. "By the way, isn't Manning on radar watch?"

"Yes, sir," replied Tom.

"Well, it's one forty-eight. How about his standard check-in with traffic control?"

Tom stammered, "He—uh—he may be plotting some space junk, sir."

"He *still* must report, regardless of what he's doing!"

"I—uh—ah—yes, sir!" gulped Tom. Blast Roger anyway, he thought, forgetting the all-important quarter-hour check-in.

"I'd better go up and find out if anything's wrong," said Connel.

"Gosh, sir," suggested Tom, desperately seeking an excuse for his shipmate. "I'm sure Roger would have notified us if anything had happened."

"Knowing Manning as I do, I'm not so sure!" And the irascible officer thundered through the door like a jet-propelled tank!

"Come on, Mason. Hurry and put on that space suit," barked Loring.

"Take it easy," grumbled Mason. "I'm working as fast as I can!"

"Of all the rotten luck," growled Loring. "Who'd ever figure the *Annie Jones* would blast off from Venus—and then stop at the space station!"

"Shows you ain't so smart," retorted Mason. "Lots of ships do that. They carry just enough fuel to get 'em off the surface, so they'll be light while they're blasting out of Venus' gravity. Then they stop at the space station to refuel for the long haul."

"All right," barked Loring, "lay off the lecture! Just get that space suit on in a hurry!"

"Listen, wise guy," challenged Mason, "just tell me one thing. If we bail out of this tub in space suits, who's going to pick us up?"

"We're not bailing out!" said Loring.

"We're not? Then what are we suiting up for?"

"Just in case," said Loring. "Now listen to me. In a few minutes the *Annie Jones*'ll make contact with traffic control. Only instead of talking to the pilot—they'll be talking to us. Because we'll have taken over."

"But unless we land they'll be suspicious. And if we land ..."

Loring interrupted. "Nobody's going to suspect a thing. I'll tell traffic control we've got an extra-heavy load. Then they won't let us land. We follow their orders and blast off into space—find an emergency fuel station—head for Tara—and nobody suspects anything."

Mason twisted his face into a scowl. "Sounds awful risky to me," he muttered.

"Sure it's risky," sneered Loring, "but you don't hit the jackpot without ever taking a *chance*!"

The two men, huddled against a jumble of packing cases in the cargo hold of the *Annie Jones*, made careful preparations. Checking their weapons, they opened their way toward the freighter's control deck. Just outside the hatch they stopped, paralo-ray guns ready, and listened.

Inside, Pilot James Jardine and Leland Bangs, his first officer, were preparing for the landing at the space station.

"Ought to be picking up the approach radar signal pretty soon," said Bangs. "Better take her off automatic control, Jardine. Use the manual for close maneuvering."

"Right," answered his spacemate. "Send out a radar blip for them to pick up. I'll check the cargo and make sure it's lashed down for landing. Captain Stefens is tough when it comes to being shipshape."

The freighter blasted evenly, smoothly onward through the darkness of space in a straight line for the man-made satellite. Jardine got up from the freighter's dual-control board, picked up a portable light, and headed for the hatch leading to the cargo deck.

"He's coming," hissed Loring. "We'll take him soon's he reaches us." There was a sharp clank as the hatch opened, and Jardine's head came into view.

"Now!" yelled Loring. He swung the heavy paralo-ray gun at Jardine's head.

"What the—" exclaimed the startled spaceman. "Bangs, look out!"

He tried to avoid the blow, but Loring's gun landed on the side of his head. Jardine crumpled to the deck.

Bangs was out of his seat in a moment, at his pilot's call. The burly redheaded spaceman saw at a glance what was wrong and lunged for the hatch.

Loring stepped toward him, holding his paralo-ray.

"All right, spaceboy!" he grated. "Hold it or I'll freeze you stiff!"

Bangs stopped and stared at the gun and at Jardine who was slumped on the deck. Mason rushed past him to the controls.

"What is this?" demanded Bangs.

"An old game," explained Loring with a sneer. "It's called 'You've got it and I take it.' And if you don't like it, you get it." He gestured with his gun. "You get it—with this."

Bangs nodded. "O.K.," he said. "O.K. But how about letting me take care of my buddy. He's hurt."

"Just a bump on the head," said Loring. "He'll come out of it soon enough."

"Hey," shouted Mason, "I can't figure out these controls!"

Loring growled angrily. "Here, lemme at them!" He forced Bangs to lie down on the deck, and then, keeping the gun trained on the redheaded spaceman, stepped quickly to the control board. He handed Mason the gun.

"Keep an eye on them while I figure this baby out."

"Least you coulda done is steal a decent ship," grumbled Mason. "This tub is so old it creaks!"

"Just shut your mouth and keep your eye on those guys," said the other. He began to mutter to himself as he tried to figure out the complicated controls.

Jardine was now conscious but had the presence of mind not to move. His head ached from the blow. Slowly he opened his eyes and saw his two attackers bending over the board. He saw that Bangs was lying on the deck facing him. Jardine winked at Bangs, who returned the signal. Then he began, carefully, methodically to send a Morse-code message to his companion via his winking eyes.

"O-N-L-Y—one—gun—between—them. You—take—big—fellow. I'll—charge—gun ..."

"Can't you figure this thing out either?" asked Mason, leaning over Loring's shoulder.

"Ah, this wagon is an old converted chemical burner. These controls are old as the sun. I've got to find the automatic pilot!"

"Try that lever over there," suggested Mason.

Loring reached over to grasp it, turning away from his prisoners.

"Bangs, get 'em!" shouted Jardine. The two men jumped to their feet and lunged at Loring and Mason. Loring dove to one side, losing the gun in the scramble, but as he fell, he reached for the acceleration control lever. He wrenched it out of its socket and brought it down on Bang's head, and the officer slid to the floor. Jardine, meanwhile, had Mason in a viselike grip, but again Loring used the lever, bringing it down hard on the neck of the freighter pilot. Jardine dropped to the deck.

"Thanks, Loring," gasped Mason. "That was close! Good thing we had on these space suits, or we'd have been finished. They couldn't grab onto the smooth plastic."

"Finished is right!" snarled Loring. "I told you to keep an eye on them! If they'd nabbed us we woulda wound up on the prison asteroid!"

"Loring," shouted Mason, "look!" He pointed a trembling finger at the thrust indicator. "We're blasting at full space speed—right for the station!"

"By the rings of Saturn," cried Loring, "I must've jammed the thrust when I yanked the lever out of the control board!"

"Put it back! Slow this ship down!" cried Mason, his face ashen with fear. Loring jumped to the control board and with trembling fingers tried to replace the lever in the socket.

"I can't—can't—" he panted. "We gotta pile outta here! We're heading for the station. We'll crash!"

"Come on! This way! We left the space helmets back in the cargo hold!" shouted Mason. He ran toward the open hatch leading to the companionway. Suddenly he stopped. "Hey, what about those two guys?"

"Never mind them!" shouted Loring. "Keep going. We can't do anything for them now!"

And as the two men raced toward the stern, the freighter, her powerful rockets wide open, arrowed straight toward the gleaming white structure of the space station.

"It was easy, honey," cooed Roger into the microphone on the main control panel of the space-station radar bridge.

"I switched the frequency on the station, beamed to a teleceiver trunk line on Earth, and called you up, my little space pet! Smart, huh? Now remember we have a date as soon as I get back from this important and secret mission. I could've got out of it, but they needed me badly. As much as I like you, baby, I had to go along to give the boys a break and ..."

" *Cadet Manning!*" An infuriated roar echoed in the small chamber.

"Yeah, whaddaya wan—" growled Roger, turning to see who had interrupted him. He suddenly gulped and turned pale. "Ohhhhhhhhh—good-by, baby!" He flipped the switch and stood up.

"Uh—ah—good morning, Major Connel," he stammered.

"What's going on here, Manning?" barked Connel.

"I—was—talking, sir," replied Roger.

"So I heard! But talking to whom?"

"To whom, sir?"

"That's what I said, Manning." Connel's voice dropped to a deep sarcastic purr. "To whom?"

"I was—ah—talking to Earth, sir."

"Official business, I presume?"

"You mean—official—like here on the station, sir?"

"Official, like here on the station, Manning," replied Connel in almost a kindly tone.

"No, sir."

"You failed to make your quarter-hour check to the traffic-control center, I believe?"

"Yes, sir," gulped Roger. The full realization of what he had done was beginning to dawn on him.

"And you've tampered with vital station equipment for your own personal use," added Connel. With a sinking feeling in the pit of his stomach, Roger noticed the major was strangely quiet in his interrogation. It felt like the calm before the storm.

"Yes, sir," admitted Roger, "I changed several circuits."

"Are you aware of the seriousness of your negligence, Manning?" Connel's voice began to harden.

"Yes—yes—I guess so, sir," stumbled Roger.

"Can you repair that radar so that it can be used as it was intended?"

"Yes, sir."

"Then do so immediately. There are ships in flight depending on your information and signals."

"Yes, sir," said Roger quietly. Then he added quickly, "I'd like the major to know, sir, that this is the first time this has happened."

"I have only your word for that, Manning!" Connel finally began blasting in his all too familiar roar. "Since you've done it once, I see no reason to think you couldn't have done it before or that you might not do it again!" The officer's face was now almost purple with rage. "When you've repaired that set, return to your quarters! You are confined until I decide on disciplinary action!"

Turning abruptly, Connel stormed out of the room, slamming the hatch closed behind him.

With a sigh Roger turned back to the set. With trembling fingers he reconnected the terminals and made delicate adjustments on the many dials. Finally, as power began to flow through the proper chain of circuits, the radar scanner glowed into life and the hair-thin line of light swept around the dull green surface of the scope. It had been left on a setting covering two hundred miles around the space station, and seeing the area was clear, Roger increased the range to five hundred miles. The resulting scan sent a sudden chill down his spine. A spaceship was roaring toward the station at full thrust!

Cold sweat beaded Roger's forehead as he grabbed for the microphone and called Tom.

"Radar bridge to control deck!" The words tumbled out frantically. "Tom! Tom! There's a ship heading right for the station! Bearing 098! Distance 450 miles! Coming in on full thrust! Tom, acknowledge! Quick!"

Down on the control deck, Tom had been watching a space freighter easing out of the station when Roger's voice came over the speaker in a thin scream.

"What?" he yelled. "Give me that again, Roger!"

"Spaceship bearing 098—full thrust! Range now four twenty-five!"

"By the craters of Luna," shouted Tom, "why didn't you pick her up sooner, Roger?"

"Never mind that. Contact that guy and tell him to change course! He can't brake in time now!"

"All right! Sign off!" Without waiting for a reply, Tom cut Roger off and switched to a standard space band. His voice quivering, the young cadet spoke quickly and urgently into the microphone. "Space station to spaceship approaching on orbit 098. Change course! Emergency! Reduce thrust and change course or you will crash into us!"

As he spoke, Tom watched the master screen of his scanner and saw the ship rocketing closer and closer with no change in speed or course. He realized that any action, even now, would bring the craft dangerously close to the station. Without hesitation, he flipped on the master switch of the central station communicator, opening every loud-speaker on the station to his voice.

"Attention! Attention! This is traffic-control center! Emergency! Repeat. Emergency! All personnel in and near landing ports five, six, seven, eight, and nine—decks A, B, and C—evacuate immediately to opposite side of the station. Emergency crews stand by for crash! Spaceship heading for station! May crash! Emergency—emergency!"

On the endangered decks, men began to move quickly, and in a moment the great man-made satellite was prepared for disaster. On the control deck, Tom stayed at his station, sounding the warning.

"Emergency! Emergency! All personnel prepare for crash! All personnel prepare for crash!"

CHAPTER 8

There—there!" shouted Captain Stefens into the mike aboard the jet boat circling around the station. "I think I see something bearing about seventy degrees to my left and up about twenty on the ecliptic! Do you see it, Scotty?"

Tom, in the bucket seat of the jet boat, strained his eyes but was unable to see over the control board.

Terry Scott, in a second jet boat ten miles away, answered quickly, "Yes, I think I see it, sir."

"Good!" shouted Stefens. "Maybe we've found something."

He spoke to Tom over his shoulder, keeping his eye on the floating objects in the black void of space. "Come to the starboard about one-quarter full turn, Corbett, and hold it. Then up, about twenty-five degrees."

"Aye, aye, sir," said Tom. He began to maneuver the small gnat-sized space craft to the proper position.

"That's good!" shouted Stefens. "Now hold that. Let me see. I think we've hit pay dirt."

From the right, Tom could see the red flash of the rockets of Terry Scott's jet boat, which Astro had volunteered to pilot, coming into view. As soon as order had been restored aboard the station, search parties had been sent out to look for survivors.

Carefully Tom slowed the space craft in response to Stefens' brief commands and soon came to a dead halt in space. There, hovering right above them, visible through the crystal dome of the jet boat, Tom could see two space-suited figures floating effortlessly. A moment later Scott's craft came alongside, and the two small ships were lashed together with magnetic lines. Tom and Stefens hurriedly pulled on their space helmets. They adjusted the valves regulating the oxygen supply in their suits, and Stefens slipped back the sliding top of the jet boat. Out on the hull he secured a line to a projecting ring, and ordering Tom to stand by, he pushed himself off the ship into the bottomless void of space.

Tom could see two space-suited figures floating effortlessly

The line trailing behind him, Stefens drifted toward the two helpless figures. He reached them in less than a minute, secured the line to their belts, and signaled Tom to haul in.

Near by, Terry Scott and Astro watched as the three figures were pulled to safety.

Quickly the top of the jet boat was closed, oxygen pressure in the craft was restored, and the four men took off their helmets.

"Whew!" said Loring. "I sure want to thank you for pulling us out of the deep!"

"We sure do, sir!" added Mason. Then, with a quick look at Loring, he asked softly, "Were there any other survivors?"

Stefens' face was grim. "Not one. After we untangled the mess, we found bodies of two men. It was pretty bad. A little later something was spotted on the radar, and we hoped there might be survivors. Luckily for you, we came to look!"

"By the rings of Saturn," swore Loring softly, "Jardine and Bangs were brave men. They practically forced us to pile out when they saw they were going to crack up." He turned to Mason. "Didn't they, Al?"

"Yeah, yeah, sure brave men," Al Mason agreed.

"Nothing to be done for them now, of course," said Stefens. "What happened?" He paused, and then added, "You don't have to tell me if you don't want to before you make out your report, but I'd sure like to know."

"I don't really know what happened, sir," said Loring. "We had made a deal for a ride back to Earth with Jardine and were sleeping back on the cargo deck. All of a sudden, Jardine came running in. Told us we were about to pile into the station and for us to suit up and get out. We asked him about himself, but he said he was going to stay and try to save the ship. We piled out, and—well, we saw the whole thing from out here. Like a big splash of light. It must have been pretty bad on the station, eh?"

"Plenty bad, but thanks to Cadet Corbett here, there wasn't a single injury. He warned everybody to get off that side of the station. A lot of damage but no casualties."

"Don't you have any idea what made the ship crash?" asked Tom quietly.

Loring looked at Tom but spoke to Stefens. "I told you all I know, sir. Can I expect to be questioned by everyone in the Solar Guard. Including cadets?"

Stefens bristled. "It was a civil question, Loring," he said stiffly, "but you don't have to say anything if you don't want to!"

Loring and Mason had not expected such a strong defense of the cadet, and Loring was quick to make amends. "I'm sorry—I guess I'm still a bit shaken up," he muttered.

Stefens grunted.

"It wasn't pretty, you know, watching that ship go up and not be able to do anything about it," Loring continued plaintively. "Jardine and Bangs—well, they're—they *were* sorta friends of mine."

They were silent all the way back to the station, each with his own thoughts—Stefens puzzling over the cause of the crash, Loring and Mason exchanging quick furtive glances and wondering how long their story would hold up, and Tom wondering how much Roger's changing the power circuits on the radar had to do with the crash of the ship.

"That's right," snapped Connel to the two enlisted spacemen. "I said I wanted the radar section of the communications deck closed and sealed off until further investigations. You can hook up and use one of the monitors in the traffic control meantime."

The two red-clad spacemen turned and walked away. Stefens stood to one side.

"Don't you think that's carrying things a little too far, sir?" he asked Connel.

"I'm doing this as much to protect Cadet Manning as I am to prosecute him! I want to be sure there was no connection between the crash of the *Annie Jones* and his tampering with the radar circuits!" Connel replied.

"I guess you're right, sir," replied Stefens. "Those two survivors, Loring and Mason, are having coffee in the mess if you want to talk to them."

"Did they change their story?" asked Connel.

"None at all. They were hooking a ride back to Atom City, and they were asleep in the cargo hold. Jardine, one of the pilots, came in and told them to pile out. They did."

"Ummmmh," mused Connel. "I know those two, Loring and Mason. Had a little trouble with them recently on a trip to Tara. Suspended their papers. So if they were just hooking a ride, it might be they're telling the truth!"

"I have a report here on the damage to the station, sir, if you'd like to listen to it," said Stefens, handing his superior a spool of audiotape.

"Good! Did you make out the report yourself?" asked Connel.

"Yes, sir. With the assistance of Terry Scott and Cadet Corbett."

"Good lad, that Corbett," said Connel and paused. "The whole unit is good! If it weren't for that hare-brained Manning, I'd say they had as bright a future in the Solar Guard as any unit I've seen!"

"I'll buy that, sir!" said Stefens with a smile. "That Corbett picked up traffic-control operations like a duck takes to water. And it's been a long time since Jenledge on the power deck raved about a cadet the way he does about Astro."

Connel smiled. He was reluctant to press for an investigation of the radar deck, knowing that if he did, it would mean a damaging black mark against Manning. But justice was justice, and Connel came closer to worshiping justice than anything else in space!

Connel placed the spool of tape in the audiograph and settled in a chair to listen. He didn't like the entire affair. He didn't like to think of losing a cadet of Manning's ability because of one stupid mistake. He had recommended a thorough investigation. There was no other way. If Manning was cleared of the responsibility for the crash, he was free, and it would not show up against his record. If he wasn't, however, then he'd have to pay. Yes, thought Connel to himself, as Stefens' voice began to crackle harshly on the audiograph, if Manning was guilty, then Manning would most certainly pay. Connel would see to that.

Deep in the heart of the space station, Loring and Mason were huddled over steaming cups of coffee whispering to each other cautiously.

"Want more coffee, Mason?" asked Loring.

"Who wants coffee when there's going to be a Solar Guard investigation?" whined Mason. "Suppose they find out something?"

"Relax, will ya?" muttered Loring reassuringly. "Connel doesn't suspect a thing. Besides, he has that cadet under arrest!"

"Yeah," argued Mason, "but you don't know those guys at Space Academy. All this honor stuff! It's not like a regular investigation. They don't stop digging until they dig up *real facts*! They'll find out we stowed away and ..."

Loring calmly added cream and sugar to his coffee. "They can't prove a thing. Jardine and Bangs are dead, and the ship's nothing but a pile of junk."

"They'll find out, I tell you, and now we've got murder on our hands!"

A door behind Mason suddenly opened and Stefens appeared.

"Shut up, you fool!" Loring hissed. He turned blandly to face Stefens. "Well, Captain, glad you came. I wanted to talk to you about getting us transportation back to Venusport."

"You'll have to wait for the jet liner from Earth," said Stefens. "See me in about two hours. Right now, I've got to make arrangements for the investigation of the crash."

"Sure, sir," said Loring. "Ah—say, Captain, what do you expect the investigation to turn up?"

"The true facts," replied Stefens. "Whether the crash was due to the negligence of Cadet Manning or something that happened on the ship."

"Then you really think the cadet may be responsible?" asked Loring softly.

"He admits to negligence, and the *Annie Jones* is a lot of evidence," said Stefens with a shrug, and walked out.

"There's our answer!" said Loring triumphantly. "Come on!"

"Where are we going?" asked Mason.

"We're going to have a little talk with our fall guy!"

"Ahhh, sit down, Roger," said Astro. "Everything will be O.K."

"Yeah," agreed Tom. "You're just wearing out the deck and your nerves walking back and forth like that. Everything will be O.K." Tom tried hard to keep any apprehension out of his voice.

"Nothing will make those two guys on the spaceship O.K.," said Roger. He kicked viciously at a stool and sat down on the side of his bunk.

Since the crash, Roger had been confined to his quarters, with Tom and Astro bringing him his meals. Tom had watched his unit-mate grow more and more bitter over the turn of events and was afraid Roger would do something rash.

The central communicator over the door suddenly buzzed, and the three cadets waited for the announcement.

"... Cadets Corbett and Astro report to rocket cruiser *Polaris* for indoctrination on hyperdrive—on the double—by order of Major Connel."

Tom and Astro got up. Astro found it hard to hide his eagerness to begin indoctrination on hyperdrive, and it was only his deep concern for Roger that kept him from letting out one of his bull-throated bellows.

"Take it easy, Roger," said Tom. "The investigation will be over and we'll be on our way to Tara before you know it."

"Yeah, you space Romeo," growled Astro, "crawl in the sack and rest your bones. You're lucky you can miss this."

Roger managed a weak smile. "I'll be O.K. Go ahead and learn about that hyperdrive before you explode."

There was an awkward moment while the three cadets stared at one another. The deep friendship between them didn't need to be expressed in words. Abruptly, Tom and Astro turned and left the room.

Roger stared at the closed door for a moment and then flopped on his bunk. He closed his eyes and tried to go to sleep. Whatever happened, he thought, it wouldn't do any good to knock himself out.

As he lay there thinking back to the first months at Space Academy when he had met Tom and Astro, he heard a knock on the door and he turned to see the steel hatch slide back stealthily. He jumped up.

Loring stuck his head inside the door. "You alone, Manning?" he asked.

"Yeah. Who're you?" asked Roger.

"My name's Loring, and this is my space buddy, Al Mason. We were on the *Annie Jones*."

Roger's eyes lighted up. "Then you know I'm not responsible for the crash!" said Roger.

"I wouldn't say that, kid," said Loring grimly. "I wouldn't say that at all."

"What do you mean?" demanded Roger.

"A shame"—Loring shook his head—"young fella like you winding up on the prison asteroid."

"Prison asteroid?" asked Roger stupidly.

"Yeah," grunted Loring. "Have you ever seen one of them joints, Manning? They work from noon to midnight. Then they give you synthetic food to eat, because it costs too much to haul up solid grub. Once you've been on the prison rock, you can't ever blast off again. You're washed up as a spaceman. Think you'll like that?"

"Why—why—what's that got to do with me?" asked Roger.

"Just this, kid. After the investigation they'll find out your radarscope wasn't working right. Then they'll come to me and ask me what happened aboard the *Annie Jones*."

"Well," demanded Roger, "what did happen?"

Loring glanced at Mason. "Just this, kid. Jardine and Bangs were on the teleceiver and the radar for fifteen minutes trying to pick up your beam. But there wasn't any, because you had it fouled up!"

Roger sat down on the side of the bunk and stared at the two men. If what they said was true, Roger knew there could only be one outcome to the investigation.

"Why are you telling me this?" asked Roger quietly.

"Very simple. I don't like to see *anyone* go to the prison rock!"

"Are you"—Roger hesitated—"are you suggesting that I escape?"

Loring and Mason got up and walked to the door. Loring turned back to face Roger. "I'm not suggesting anything, Manning," he said. "You're a big boy and should know what's good for you. But"—he paused and measured his words carefully—"if I were you, I wouldn't wait around for Connel or anyone else to blast my life to pieces by sending me to a prison for one little mistake!"

The hatch slid closed behind the two spacemen.

Roger stood up and began packing a small spaceman's bag. There was a jet liner coming in from Atom City that would make a stop at Venusport. He glanced at his watch. Thirty minutes. He didn't have much time.

CHAPTER 9

Attention! Attention! This is a general alert!" Tom Corbett's voice was hollow as he spoke over a solar-wide audiocast. "Wanted! Space Cadet Roger Manning. Five feet, eleven inches tall, one hundred sixty-five pounds. Blue eyes. Blond hair. Last seen wearing dress blues. Cadet Manning broke confinement to quarters on Venus space station and is believed to be heading back to Earth. He is wanted in connection with the crash of the space freighter *Annie Jones* and the death of two spacemen. All information regarding the whereabouts of Manning should be forwarded to Captain Isaiah M. Patrick, Senior Security Officer, Solar Guard, Space Academy, Earth. This alert is to be transmitted to all local authorities."

Tom snapped the switch off and silently watched the glowing audio tubes darken. He turned to one side and saw Astro. The big Venusian was seated on a desk, slumped over, his head held in his massive hands.

"You know," said Astro slowly, "I could take that guy Manning and break him in two for running out!"

Tom didn't answer. When they had discovered that Roger was missing it had been a terrific blow. Unaware that Roger, in his confused state of mind, had been an easy victim to Loring and Mason's trickery and had innocently walked into their trap, the two cadets felt that his escape was a breach of trust. Roger had given his spaceman's word that he would confine himself to his quarters. Roger had broken that trust, and now the fact was being flashed around the entire solar system; Roger Manning was an escaped criminal!

"There's nothing we can do now," said Tom. "The whole universe knows it. He's finished! Washed up! The only thing that could save him now would be absolute clearance by the investigation. But since he's run out, I guess it must be the other way around. He was afraid he was going to get caught." Tom's voice was cold and bitter. "And we can't blame anyone but—"

"*But Manning!*" barked a voice behind them. Astro jumped up and snapped to attention. Tom turned to see Major Connel stride into the room. It was at Connel's insistence that Tom had been ordered to broadcast the alert for Roger.

"That's the last time I ever want to hear any sympathy for a man who broke his word!" snarled Connel.

"I have something I'd like to say to the major," said Astro in a deliberate voice, "as man to man!"

Even at attention, Tom jerked his head involuntarily to look at Astro. Connel's eyes narrowed. "Here it comes," he thought. "Well, I've handled rebellion of this sort before." He stepped close to Astro. So close in fact that the black and gold of his uniform brushed the massive chest of the cadet from Venus.

"You have permission to speak, man to man!" snapped Connel.

Astro paused for a moment. Then he relaxed and brought his eyes down to the level of the major.

"I am a human being, sir," said Astro in the deepest voice Tom had ever heard. It was strong and full of emotion, yet controlled. "And as long as I am a human being, I shall consider Roger Manning one of the finest men I'll ever know."

"Are you finished?" snapped Connel.

"No, sir, I'm not," said Astro. "I speak in defense of the man, the *spaceman*, not the uniform, or the trust he betrayed. And I respectfully request of the major that if his feelings for Cadet Manning are so violent that he finds it difficult to control them, that he make a special effort to control them"—Astro paused and stuck out his chin—"in my presence!"

Connel stepped back. "And if I don't?" he shouted.

"Then I shall ask for a transfer from your command, sir, and if that is not granted, then I shall resign from the Academy."

"And?" asked Connel.

"And, sir—" Astro stumbled.

"*And what*, Cadet Astro?" roared Connel.

"I have nothing more to say, sir," said Astro.

Tom, who had at first had to control an impulse to laugh at the strange seriousness of Astro's manner and tone, now found it equally difficult to hold back the tears that were welling up in his eyes.

Connel was not going to let the incident stand there. He had secretly hoped that such a situation would present itself, because he wanted to see what material the *Polaris* unit was made of. And he was secretly satisfied. Any cadet who would offer to resign from the Academy in defense of his unit-mate was a true spaceman. Connel wasn't going to allow Astro or Tom to resign over some foolish trick of Roger's, but, at the same time, he couldn't allow them to take too many liberties with discipline. Connel turned to Tom.

"I suppose you feel the same way, Corbett?" he asked.

"I do, sir," said Tom.

"Of course you know I could make your lives miserable now," he threatened.

"We are aware of that, sir," said Tom quietly.

"Very well, Cadets Corbett and Astro. I shall comply with your request. Not because of your request but out of respect for your feelings as spacemen. I wouldn't have thought much of you if you hadn't come out in defense of Manning. And just for your own sake, Astro," said Connel, stepping back in front of the big cadet, "never ask to talk to a Solar Guard officer man to man again. As long as you're still a member of the Cadet Corps such disrespect will not be tolerated. Another man, who might not have understood your feelings, could have used your desire for fair play as a means of trapping you into one of the worst offenses in the Spaceman's Code—striking a Solar Guard officer!"

"Yes, sir," mumbled Astro. "Thank you, sir."

"Report aboard the *Polaris*"—Connel glanced at his watch—"in fifteen minutes. I'm going to put you through your paces on hyperdrive and the operation of the transmitter."

"Then we're still going to make the trip to Tara, sir?" asked Tom.

"We certainly are, Corbett," replied Connel. "In two hours another cadet is arriving from the Academy to replace Roger. His name's Alfie Higgins. Perhaps you know him."

Tom smiled. "Yes, sir, we know him," he replied. "Cadet Higgins is a friend of mine. He carries the nickname of 'The Brain.' Has the highest I.Q. in the Academy."

"Good. I'm glad you know him, because this is going to be a rough trip. We got off to a bad start, but it's all over now. So forget it. And before I go, I want you to know this. In my personal opinion, Manning had nothing to do with the crash. I think the whole trouble was caused on the ship. I have nothing to back up my opinion, except my feelings. But feelings can go a long way in making a man innocent until proved guilty. Unit dis-missed!"

Alfie Higgins listened attentively to the story of the crash and Roger's disappearance as Tom, and then Astro, described the situation in detail.

"It is a pity, of course, but Manning was always the impulsive type. Not very definite in his attitude and emotionally unstable," commented Alfie when the story was finished.

"Lay off that talk, you overstuffed brain!" growled Astro. "In this outfit, Roger is just away on vacation!"

"Yes—yes, of course!" said Alfie quickly. It wasn't wise to get off on the wrong foot in a new unit, especially when one was trying to fill the shoes of a cadet, who, Alfie had to admit, had everything. Alfie Higgins' mother didn't raise any stupid children, he said to himself. He was too happy being a member of the *Polaris* unit, the hottest crew at the Academy, to allow anything to interfere with his success.

"I've heard a great deal about hyperdrive," he said quickly, changing the subject. "I would appreciate it if you could describe the basis of this new feature in space travel so that I may have at least a surface familiarity with its operation and application."

Astro gulped and looked at Tom. "Might as well get used to that kind of chatter, Astro," said Tom, smiling. "Alfie can't talk any other way."

"Is there something wrong with the way I speak?" asked Alfie, wrinkling up his nose a little to see through the thick lenses of his glasses.

"You wanta know about hyperdrive?" growled Astro.

"To be sure, if you'd be so kind," said Alfie.

"Well, if you'll close your trap long enough, I'll tell you about it!"

Alfie sat back and waited, hands clasped around one knee.

"In the first place," began Astro, "hyperdrive was developed by Joan Dale back at the Academy. And it's so blasted simple, I get mad at myself for not thinking of it first!"

"Uhhh," snorted Alfie. "I respect your great talent on the power deck, Astro, but I would hardly compare myself with Dale!"

"Shut up!" barked Astro. "You'll see how simple it is! Hyperdrive is based on the idea that the thrust of the rockets acts in the exact same way on *all* the atoms inside the spaceship. So you can have as much thrust as you want and no one will feel a thing. Even if the ship were to accelerate a million times faster than the gravity of the Earth you wouldn't feel a thing, because all the atoms inside would be pushed along at the same time!" Astro sat back triumphantly.

"Ummmmh," commented Alfie. "That sounds all right as a principle, but will it work out in space?"

"Listen, you—you—" snorted Astro.

"Sure it will, Alfie," said Tom. "It's been tested before."

"Still room for improvement, though," commented Alfie.

"I'll improve your head," barked Astro, "if you don't close that big mouth! How do you like that, Tom? We get rid of one space-gassing Romeo and now we get one even worse!"

Astro's reference to Roger made Tom draw a quick breath. In the short while since Alfie's arrival and the week since Roger's disappearance there hadn't been time to forget their old unit-mate and get accustomed to a new personality. Astro sensed Tom's feelings and irritably banged one hamlike fist into the other. Alfie was O.K., thought the big Venusian, but by the craters of Luna, he wasn't Roger.

"Attention—attention!" The intercom crackled into life. "*Polaris* unit—by order of Major Connel—stand by to blast off immediately. This is first warning! Pack your gear and stand by to blast off immediately."

Tom, Astro, and Alfie got up, and with the image of Roger fresh in their minds, made their way to the landing-port deck where the great gleaming spaceship was slung on magnetic cradles. They were met at the hatch by Major Connel.

"All right," he said, "we leave all thoughts of Manning right here on the station. I know it's tough, but we've got a still tougher job to do. This is to be a scientific expedition and we'll need every ounce of energy and intelligence we have—*collectively*—to make a success of this mission. Cadet Corbett!"

"Yes, sir," replied Tom.

"Stand by to blast off in five minutes!"

CHAPTER 10

C an I speak with you a minute, spaceman?"

Roger turned from the automatic food dispenser and stared at a wizened little man standing beside him, grinning up at him toothlessly.

"What do you want?" asked Roger.

"Just talk. Let's sit down at this table, eh?" said the little man, taking the cadet by the arm. "Gotta little deal I think you might be interested in."

Roger cast a quick appraising glance over the shabbily dressed man and walked to the table. Unless someone knew Roger personally, it would have been hard to recognize him. No longer wearing the vivid blue of the senior Space Cadet, he was now dressed in black trousers fitting snugly around the legs, a midnight blue pull-over jersey, and the black-billed hat of the merchant spaceman. His once close-cropped blond hair was beginning to grow shaggy around the edges, and with the hat pulled low over his forehead, he might have been another person entirely.

Leaving the space station on the jet liner had been easy for Roger, since no one suspected he would violate his trust. But once his absence was discovered and the warrant issued for his arrest, it had been necessary for him to assume some sort of disguise to elude the Solar Guard MP's. Roger had wound up on Spaceman's Row in Venusport as a matter of course. Luckily, when he left the station, he had the foresight to take all of his money with him, so he was not yet in need.

On Spaceman's Row, Roger found the new freedom from discipline enjoyable at first, but now the novelty had worn off. Having visited all of the interesting places on the Row, existence there had become boring. His one attempt to leave Spaceman's Row had nearly met with disaster. Running into a squad of Solar Guard MP's, he had made a hurried escape into a near-by jet taxi. Back on the Row, Roger had lounged around the cafes, feeling the loneliness that haunts men wanted by the law. And only because he was so lonely he had agreed to talk to the little man who sat and stared at him from across the table.

"You a rocket pusher, astrogator, or skipper?" asked the little man.

"Who wants to know?" asked Roger cautiously.

"Look, sonny boy," was the quick retort. "I'm Mr. Shinny! I'm the fixer of Spaceman's Row. You want something, come to me and I'll get it for you. I don't care why you're here. That ain't none of my business. But the fact remains that you're here, and you don't come down here unless you're in trouble space deep!"

Roger looked at the little man more closely. "Suppose I am in something deep? What could you do for me?" he asked.

"What would you want done?" asked Shinny slyly.

"Well," said Roger casually, "I could use a set of papers."

"What happened to your own?"

"Solar Guard picked them up," answered Roger simply.

"For what?" asked Shinny.

"Taking ice cream away from the skipper's pet monkey!" snapped Roger.

Shinny threw back his head and laughed. "That's good—very good!" He wiped his mouth after spitting at a near-by cuspidor. He reached over and patted Roger on the arm. "You'll do, sonny! You'll do right well on the Row. Join me in a little acceleration sport?"

"What's that?" asked Roger.

"Rocket juice!" said Shinny. "Ain't you never heard of rocket juice?"

"I've heard about it," said Roger with a smile, "and I'm still here to talk about it because I never drank any of it." Roger liked the little man for some reason—he couldn't tell why. He had met several people on the Row since his arrival, but they had all wanted to know how many credits he had and where he was staying.

"I took a jolt of that stuff once in Luna City," said Roger. "I was ready to blast off without a rocket ship!"

Shinny laughed again. "Good lad! Well, you won't mind if I have just a little one?" He paused and wiped his lips. "On you, of course!"

"One"—Roger held up his finger—"on me, of course!"

"Hey, there!" yelled Shinny. "You, with the asteroid head! Gimme a short bucket of that juice and bring a bottle of Martian fizz along with it!" The bartender nodded, and Shinny turned back to Roger. "Martian fizz is nothing more than a little water with sugar in it," he explained.

"Yeah, I know," replied Roger. "What about those papers?"

"I'll talk to you, spaceman to spaceman," said Shinny, "when you're ready to talk to me, spaceman to spaceman!"

They were silent while the bartender slopped a glass full of bluish liquid in front of Shinny and the bottle of Martian fizz and a glass in front of Roger. Roger paid for the drinks and poured a glass of the mild sweet water. Sipping it silently, he suddenly put the glass down again and looked Shinny in the eye.

"You know who I am," he stated quietly.

"Yep!" replied Shinny. "You're Roger Manning, Space Cadet! Breach of honor and violation of the Spaceman's Oath. Escaped from the Venus space station on a jet liner. But one of the best men on a radar scanner and astrogation prism in the whole alliance!" Shinny related the information rapidly.

"He had known all the time," thought Roger. "He was testing me." Roger wondered why.

"What are you going to do about it?" questioned Roger, thinking about the one-thousand-credit reward, standard price offered by the Solar Guard for all wanted men.

"If I had wanted to, I could have bought the finest jet liner in space with money made on Solar Guard rewards," snapped Shinny. "We got our own spaceman's code here on the Row. It goes something like this. What a man wants to bring with him down here, he brings. What he don't bring, don't exist!"

Roger smiled and stuck out his hand. "All right, Mr. Shinny! I want a set of papers—space papers! Made out in any name, so that I can get out into space again. I don't care where I go or on what, or how long I'm gone. I just gotta blast off!"

"You want papers for the astrogation deck, or control, or as a power pusher?" asked Shinny.

Roger thought a moment. "Better make them for the control deck," he said.

"Credits," said Shinny. "You have any credits?"

"How much?" asked Roger.

"One hundred now," said Shinny, and then added, "and one hundred when I deliver."

"Guaranteed papers?"

"Positively!" snorted Shinny. "I don't sell things that ain't good! I'm an honest man!"

Roger reached inside his jersey and pulled out a small roll of crumpled credit notes. He counted off one hundred and handed them over to Shinny.

"When do I get the papers?" asked Roger.

"Tomorrow, same place, same time," answered Shinny.

"What's the name of this place?" asked Roger.

"Cafe Cosmos."

Roger picked up his glass of sweet water, raising it in a toast to the little man in front of him. "Until tomorrow, Mr. Shinny, when you come here with the papers, or I come looking for you with bare knuckles!"

"You don't scare me!" snapped Shinny. "I'll be here!"

Roger tilted his chair back and smiled his casual smile. "I know you'll be back, Mr. Shinny. You see, I really mean what I say. And more important, *you* know I mean what I say!"

Shinny got up. "Tomorrow, same time, same place," he said, hurrying out the door.

Roger finished the bottle of Martian fizz, suddenly very depressed. He didn't really want the false papers. He just wanted to get away from the deadly humdrum existence on Spaceman's Row. He walked wearily back to his scrubby little bedroom to wait for night to come. He hated to go back to the room, because he knew he would think about Tom and Astro and the Space Academy. Now he couldn't allow himself to think about it any more. It was past. Finished.

"You got *who*?" asked Loring.

"I said I got the best astrogator in the deep for ya!" snapped Shinny.

Loring looked at Mason and then suddenly burst out laughing, dropping his head on the table.

"What's the matter with you?" demanded Shinny. "You got space fever or something?"

Mason, sitting quietly in the dirty hotel room, was grinning from ear to ear.

"So you got Manning for us, eh?" repeated Loring at last. "I wanta tell you something, Shinny. I was the one that got that kid to break outta that space station!"

"You what?" asked Shinny. The little spaceman had come to like the straight-forwardness of Roger.

"That's right," said Loring. "When Mason and me loused up taking over the *Annie Jones*, that kid, Manning, was on the radar watch at the station. At the same time we were gonna crash into the station he crossed a coupla wires and was talking to his girl back on Earth! They think *he* fouled up the radar and caused the crash!"

"Then he's your fall guy," commented Shinny thoughtfully.

"Right," said Loring. "And now you come along and tell us that we can get him to astrogate us out to Tara! I tell ya, Mason, this is the greatest gag I've heard in years!"

"Yeah," agreed Mason, his weak mouth still stretched in a stupid grin, "but you have to be careful he never finds out it was us that got him into all his trouble!"

"Leave that to me," said Loring. "He'll never know a thing. In fact, he'll thank us for getting him off the station and then giving him a chance to get back in space." He turned to Shinny. "You got the ship?"

"I told you before," said Shinny, "there ain't anything to be had."

"Well, we gotta have a ship," said Loring. "A fortune waiting for us in the deep and no space wagon to go get it!"

"There *is* a ship," said Shinny. "Not too good, but a spaceship."

"Where?" asked Loring.

"Near Venusport. Out in the jungles, to be exact. Needs a little fixing, but it'll make a deep space hop well enough."

"Who does it belong to?" demanded Loring.

"Me," said Shinny, a strange twinkle in his eyes.

"*You?*" gasped Loring. "By the craters of Luna, where did you get a spaceship?"

"Fifteen years ago a freighter was forced down in the jungles right near Venusport," said Shinny. "I was prospecting near by for pitchblende, back when everybody thought Venus was loaded with it. I saw the crew leave in jet boats. Soon as they was out of sight I went over to take a look. I wanted to see if there was any grub I could swipe and save myself a trip back to Venusport for more supplies. Anyway, I went aboard and found the grub all right, but I got nosy about why they had made an emergency touchdown. I looked around the power deck and found they had busted their reaction timer. I got the idea then of fixing it up and bringing it back to Venusport to give them young jerks a surprise. I lifted her off the ground and then figured why should I give it back? Just move it someplace else and let the vines and creepers grow over it for a few days."

"Didn't the crew come back looking for it?" asked Loring.

"Did they?" chortled Shinny. "I'll say they did! Almost drove them poor fellers crazy. I guess they searched for that old wagon for three months before giving up."

"And—and you mean it's still there—and in good condition?" asked Loring.

"Needs a little fuel," said Shinny, "and probably a good overhaul, but I don't think there's anything serious the matter with it."

"By the craters of Luna," exclaimed Loring, "we'll blast off immediately!"

"Hold on," said Shinny. "I didn't say I'd give it to you."

"Well, what do you want for it?" demanded Loring.

"Now let me see," mused Shinny. "I figure that if *you* figure to get as much as twenty million credits out of the copper, a full quarter share ought to be about right."

"Five million credits for a—a ship that's been rotting in the jungle for fifteen years!" exclaimed Loring.

"She's in good shape," defended Shinny. "I go out there every six months or so and turn over the reactors just to keep 'em from getting rusty."

"Why didn't you try to do something with it before?" asked Loring.

"Never had no occasion to," answered Shinny. "Well, is it a deal, or isn't it?"

"Too much," snapped Loring.

"That's my price," said Shinny.

"I could take the ship and not give you anything," sneered Loring.

"If the Solar Guard looked for three months in that jungle, with a hundred men and instruments, do you think you'll find it?"

"I'll give you a fifth share," said Loring.

"Nope," said Shinny, "I've named my price. You either take it or leave it!" He glared at Loring.

Mason finally spoke. "Take it, Loring," he said, "and let's get out of here. I'm getting jittery over that investigation that's coming up on the station."

"All right," said Loring, "it's a deal. One quarter share for the ship."

"Done!" said Shinny—"Now I guess we'd better go talk to that boy Manning, eh?"

"Don't you think it'll be a little dangerous taking him along?" whined Mason.

"Yeah, maybe you're right," said Loring.

"If it was me," said Shinny, "I wouldn't give it a second thought. You're going into ***deep*** space. It ain't like a hop to Mars or Titan. This is as deep as you can go. If I was you, I'd want the best there is in my crew. And from what I've heard about that young feller, he's the best there is on the radar bridge. You know who his father was?"

"Who?" asked Mason.

"Ken—" Shinny suddenly closed his mouth tight. "Just another spaceman," he said, "but a good one!" He rose quickly. "Well, I'm supposed to meet Manning in an hour at the Cosmos."

The three men left the dingy hotel and walked out into the main street of Spaceman's Row. In a few moments they arrived at the Cafe Cosmos. Roger was already there, seated at the same table and watching the door. When he saw Loring and Mason with Shinny, he eyed them warily.

"Hiya, kid!" greeted Loring. "Glad to see you took my advice and got away from

'Blast-off' Connel." Mason waved a salute, and the three men sat down.

Roger ignored Loring and Mason, speaking directly to Shinny. "Did you complete our deal?" he asked softly.

"Nope," answered Shinny. "I brought you another one instead."

Roger held out his hand. "My one hundred credits—*now!*"

"Never mind the credits, kid," said Loring, "we've got more important things to talk about."

Roger continued to look at Shinny, his palm outstretched on the top of the table. "One hundred credits," he repeated coldly.

Reluctantly, Shinny handed over the money. Slowly, carefully, Roger counted the bills, and then, after putting them away, he turned to face Loring for the first time.

"You said you have something important to discuss with me?" he drawled.

"I see you learned fast, kid!" said Loring with a crooked smile. "I wouldn't trust Shinny as far as I could throw a comet!"

Mason laughed loudly. The other three merely glared at him, and he stopped abruptly.

"Here's the proposition, Manning," said Loring, leaning across the table. "I've gotta ship and I wanta make a hop into deep space. I want you to do the astrogation!"

"I'm interested," said Roger. "Keep talking."

Briefly Loring described the copper satellite, its potential value, and what they expected to get out of it. Roger listened without comment. When Loring had finished, Shinny told him about the ship and its condition. When Shinny finished, Loring turned to Roger.

"Well, Manning," he asked, "how do you like the setup?"

"How much do I get out of it?" asked Roger.

"One twentieth of the take," said Loring.

"There are four of us. One full quarter-share, nothing less," drawled Roger.

"One-fourth to Shinny and one-fourth to him," whined Mason. "That only leaves us a fourth apiece!"

"That's more than you've got now," snapped Loring. "All right, Manning, you're in!"

Roger smiled for the first time. "When do we blast off?"

"As soon as we get that space wagon in shape we hit the deep!" said Loring.

"I think I need a drink on that," said Shinny. He yelled for the bartender, who brought rocket juice and Martian fizz.

Roger picked up the glass of the sweet water and glanced around the table.

"What's the name of that space wagon you've got buried in the jungles, Mr. Shinny?"

"Ain't got no name," said Shinny.

Roger paused, a slight smile playing at the corners of his mouth. "Then I propose we name her after the hearts of each of us here at the table."

"What's that?" asked Loring.

"*Space Devil*," said Roger.

Shinny grinned, his frail body trembling slightly from his silent laughter. He held up the glass of rocket juice.

"I propose a toast to the *Space Devil*!"

"To the *Space Devil*," said the others together.

"And whatever trouble she brings," added Roger softly.

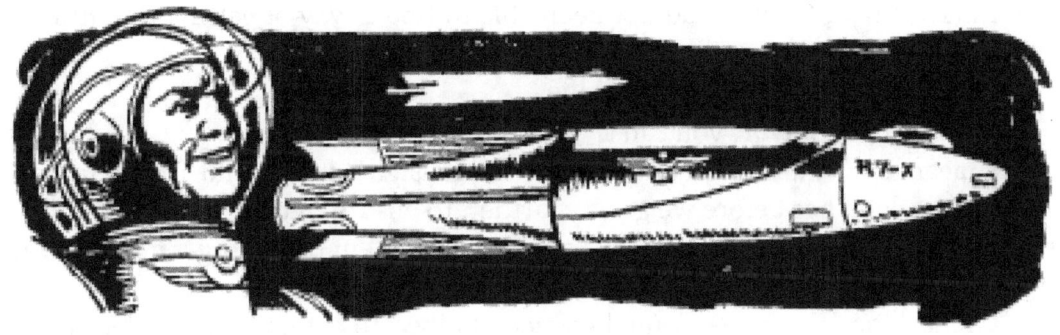

CHAPTER 11

C adet *Higgins*!" Major Connel's voice roared over the ship's intercom as the giant rocket cruiser *Polaris* blasted smoothly through space.

"Yes, sir," squeaked Alfie in reply.

"Cadet Higgins," said Connel, "I thought I had requested a sight on the sun star Regulus at fifteen hundred hours!"

"You did, sir," replied Alfie.

" ***Then why, by the craters of Luna, don't I have that position?***"

"I was—busy, sir," came the meek reply.

"Cadet Higgins," sighed Connel patiently, "would you be so kind as to come down to the control deck?"

In the short space of time since their departure from the space station Major Connel had learned that to scold Cadet Higgins was not the way to gain his attention. In fact, Major Connel had not been able to find a way of getting the little cadet's attention in any manner, at any time, on anything.

"I can't right now, sir," replied Alfie.

"What do you ***mean***, you can't?" exploded Connel.

"I mean, sir," explained Alfie, "that I've just sighted Tara and I have to get a position check on her before we go any farther, to ensure that we traverse the same trajectory on our return trip and thus avoid the problem of finding a new and safe route back."

"Cadet Alfie Higgins"—Connel's voice climbed to a frenzied shriek—"if you are not on this control deck in ten seconds, I'll personally see that you are fed to a dinosaur when we touch down on Tara and you'll never return. ***Now get down here!***"

Tom and Astro, who could hear the conversation over the intercom, were finding it very difficult to keep from laughing out loud at the innocence of Alfie and the outraged wrath of Major Connel.

Tom, particularly, had discovered that Alfie's innocent refusal to be bullied by Connel had made the time pass more quickly on the long haul through deep space. More than once he had seen Major Connel rage against the underweight cadet and become even more frustrated at his childlike resistance. It had helped Tom forget the empty feeling he experienced every time he called the radar deck and heard Alfie's mild voice instead of Roger's usual mocking answer. Astro, too, had managed to forget the loneliness he felt aboard the great cruiser by watching the antics of Alfie and Major Connel. More than once he had instigated situations where Alfie would get caught red-handed in a harmless error, and then he lay flat on the power deck, laughing until his sides ached, as he listened to Alfie and Major Connel over the intercom.

It had helped. Both Tom and Astro admitted it had helped, but it still didn't take away the dull ache each felt when an occasional remark, situation, or thought would bring Roger to mind.

Tom flipped the teleceiver on and waited for the blank screen to show him Tara. Connel stood to one side, also watching for the image of the planet to take form on the gray-black screen. A hatch clanked behind them, and Alfie stepped into the control deck to snap to his version of attention.

"Cadet Higgins reporting, sir," he said quietly.

Connel stepped in front of him, placed his hands on his hips, and bent slightly, pushing his face almost into Alfie's.

"Cadet Higgins, I want you to know I have taken all the blasted space-brained antics I'm going to take from you," said Connel quietly.

"Yes, sir," replied Alfie blandly.

"And," said Connel, shaking a finger in Alfie's face, "*and* if there is one more—just *one* more brazen, flagrant disregard of my *specific* orders, then, Cadet Higgins, I promise you the most miserable trip back to Earth you will ever know in your entire career! I promise you I'll make you sweat! I'll—I'll—" Connel stopped short and shuddered. Alfie's owl-eyed look of innocence seemed to unnerve him. He tried to resume his tirade, but the words failed him. He finally turned away, growling, "Higgins, get up on that radar deck and do as you're told, *when* you're told to do it and *not* when you want to do it! Is that clear?"

"Yes, sir," said Alfie meekly. He saluted and returned to the radar deck.

"Corbett!" snapped Connel. "If I should appear to be losing control of myself when addressing Cadet Higgins, you have my official permission to restrain me. Use force if necessary!"

Tom bit his lip to keep from laughing and managed to mumble "Yes, sir." He turned quickly to the control board and began focusing on the planet lying dead ahead of the decelerating spaceship. They had been slowing down for several days, since their speed with the added hyperdrive had been increased greatly. The young cadet adjusted the last dial and the blue-green planet sprang into clear sharp focus on the screen.

"Why," gasped Tom. "Sir, look! It's just like Earth!"

"In more ways than one, Corbett," replied Connel. "What's our range?"

"I'd say we're close enough to reduce thrust to a quarter regular space speed, sir."

"Very well," said Connel. "Now look to the right on the screen. See that small dark patch over there in the middle of the planet?"

"Yes, sir," replied Tom.

"That's where we want to touch down," said Connel. "You stay here on the control deck and maneuver the ship closer in while I go to the radar deck and contact Space Academy on the transmitter. I've got to report that we expect to land soon."

"Very well, sir," said Tom. He turned and flipped the intercom switch. "Control deck to power deck," he said. "Check in, Astro."

"Power deck here," replied Astro. "What's up, Tom?"

"We just got our first good look at Tara. She's dead ahead. Major Connel's going to contact Space Academy, and I'm going to maneuver into our preliminary glide. Stand by for course changes."

"Make it an easy touchdown. I wanta get home, you know," replied Astro good-naturedly.

"O.K.," said Tom. "Better bring her down to one-quarter space speed."

"Hyper or regular?" asked Astro.

"Regular!" yelled Tom. "You give me a quarter on hyper and we'll go right through that planet!"

"One-quarter regular space speed," replied Astro.

Tom adjusted his controls for the speed reduction, while keeping his eyes on the teleceiver screen. He watched the planet grow larger before his eyes, and the terrain become more distinct. He could see two large oceans, the green-blue of the water reflecting the sunlight of Alpha Centauri brilliantly. Nearer and nearer the *Polaris* plummeted, and Tom could begin to distinguish the rough outline of mountain ranges along the horizon line. He switched to a larger view of the planet on the magnascope that revealed a splendor rivaling the beauty of his own cherished Earth.

"We'll be entering the atmosphere in a minute, Alfie," yelled Tom into the intercom. "Stand by to give range for touchdown."

"Radar deck, aye," reported Alfie. "Range at present five hundred miles."

"Power deck, check in!" yelled Tom.

"Power deck, aye," returned Astro.

"All set below?" asked Tom.

"All set," said Astro.

"Reduce thrust to minimum!" shouted Tom.

Deep inside the powerful ship, the roar of the mighty atomic rocket motors began to fade to a deep growling purr.

"Control deck to radar deck. Major Connel, sir?"

"What is it, Corbett?" asked Connel.

"We're ready for a touchdown. Do you want to take over the bridge?"

"Can't you do it, Corbett?" asked Connel.

"Yes, sir!" replied Tom.

"Then carry on," replied Connel. "I'm having some trouble trying to get through to the Academy on the transmitter. Can't understand it." There was a pause. "I have them now, Corbett! You carry on!" he shouted.

"Aye, aye, sir," said Tom. He turned his attention to the control panel, checking the many dials and gauges with one sweeping glance, and then concentrated on bringing the ship to a safe landing on the foreign planet. His fingers tingled as he reached for the switches that would bring the ship down on the first intergalactic world he had ever visited. In a flash, the curly-haired cadet remembered childhood dreams of doing just what he was doing at this moment, preparing to touch down on a new world, millions of miles away from his home near New Chicago.

"Range one hundred miles," reported Alfie over the intercom.

"Power deck, reduce thrust to absolute minimum!" ordered Tom. "I want as little sustaining power as you can give me without cutting out altogether, Astro."

"Can do!" said Astro. The ship slowed even more, then suddenly picked up speed again as the gravity of Tara began to tug at the space traveler.

"Stand by to fire braking rockets!" yelled Tom. He was all nerves now, sensitive to the throbbing of the great ship's motors, eyes fastened to the dials and meters on the control panel. There was no time to watch the scanner view of the onrushing planet now. He had to touch down blindly, using only his instruments. "Radar bridge, report!" snapped Tom.

"Range one thousand feet," reported Alfie, his calm voice in striking contrast to the nervous excitement in Tom's. "Seven hundred fifty—six hundred—five fifty—"

"Fire braking rockets!" rasped Tom into the intercom.

The great ship bucked under the sudden thrust of the huge braking rockets. The *Polaris* held steady for a moment, then gradually, as the pull of Tara began again, she settled back toward the dark-green jungles beneath her.

"Two hundred and fifty feet," reported Alfie. "One hundred and seventy-five—one fifty—" he droned.

"Ease her up, Astro," shouted Tom. "Easy! Ease her up, you Venusian clunk, we're dropping too fast!"

Once again, from the heart of the *Polaris*, there came a roaring blast of the powerful motors. The ship steadied once more and then slipped back into her fall toward the new planet under more sure control.

"Fifty feet," reported Alfie. "Forty—thirty—twenty—"

There was a brief pause, as if everything had stopped and they were held still by a giant hand, and then, suddenly, a rocking motion, a slight bump and rumble. Tom knew they were down.

"*Touchdown!*" he yelled at the top of his voice. "Touchdown! We made it—we made it!"

From the power deck, quiet except for the whining of the oxygen feed pump,

Astro's bellow could be heard vibrating through the passageways.

"*Yeeeeeeeeeeeeeooooooooooooooowwwwwwww!*"

Tom began shutting off the many circuits and switches and made a quick last-minute check of the now dead ship. Satisfied, he glanced at the great solar clock, noted the time in the log, and stepped to the ladder leading to the radar bridge.

"Cadet Corbett reporting, sir," said Tom, saluting smartly. "I wish to report, sir, that the *Polaris* made touchdown on the planet Tara at exactly seventeen fifty-nine, solar time!"

Connel, his great bulk bent over the tiny transmitter, was twirling the dials, his head encased in a vacuum earphone helmet to ensure perfect silence. He had acquired the knowledge of lip reading out of necessity on the power decks of the old chemical burners thirty years before, and while he couldn't hear what Tom had said, he knew what the report was.

"Very well, Corbett," he shouted, not being able to judge the volume of his voice. "Good job! Can't seem to pick them up at the Academy again. Had them once, then lost them. Am placing you in command of an expedition for a quick look outside. Arm yourselves with paralo-ray guns and rifles. Take a jet boat and under no circumstances are you to land. Dismissed! Oh, yes, one more thing. Take Alfie Higgins along with you and keep *your eye on him*. Report back in one hour!"

Tom felt a tingle of excitement run up his backbone as he heard the tough skipper give him permission to explore the planet.

He saluted and turned away, Alfie trailing him down the ladder.

"Hey, Astroooo!" yelled Tom. "Get number-one jet boat out of the hatch. We're going for a look-see at this place!"

Tom went to the gun locker and took out three paralo-ray guns and rifles. He made sure each of them was fully loaded and then handed them to Alfie.

"Put these on the jet boat, Alfie. I'll be along in a minute."

Alfie took the guns and walked toward the jet-boat catapult deck. Tom returned to the radar bridge and stood before Connel.

"Would you see if there is any news of Roger, sir, when you make contact with the Academy?"

Connel read the cadet's lips and nodded his head. Tom turned and went directly to the jet-boat deck. Astro and Alfie waited for him inside.

"Brought along three space suits, Tom," said Astro. "You can never tell what we might run into."

"Good idea," said Tom.

The three cadets climbed into the jet boat, Tom taking the pilot's seat. He pushed a release button, and a portion of the *Polaris'* steel hull slid back. Tom pressed another button, gripped the wheel of the small space craft, and stepped on the acceleration pedal. The little red ship shot out of the open hatch and zoomed over the giant trees.

Traveling at a slow speed, Tom made a wide arc over the forest, checking his position against that of the *Polaris* before losing sight of it. He pulled the tiny ship up to one thousand feet, leveled off, set the automatic pilot, and took his first close look at Tara, four and a half light years from Earth.

From above, Tara seemed to be a quagmire of reptiles, dinosaurs, and dense vegetation reaching as high as the gleaming towers of Venusport and Atom City. Huge trees that spread their branches over an area of a thousand feet soared skyward, limbs and trunks wrapped in jungle creepers. Now and then Alfie would grasp Tom or Astro by the arm and point a wavering finger at a moving animal below, then gasp and fall back white-faced into his seat. While Tom was inclined to share Alfie's reactions, Astro took it in stride, having been exposed to the dangers of wild jungles on his own Venus.

The tiny jet boat raced out across the blue-green sea that swept up in giant swells along the snow-white sandy beaches. It was a temptation to set the small craft down and enjoy the pleasure of a swim after the many days of cramped, tortured living on the *Polaris*. But Tom remembered Connel's orders and also had a lot of respect for some of the things he had seen swimming in the water.

"Better get back," said Tom. He flipped the audiophone switch in the jet boat and spoke into a small mike.

"Jet boat one to *Polaris*. Jet boat one to *Polaris*. Cadet Corbett to Major Connel."

There was a crackle of static and then Connel's voice, vibrant and clear, filled the small cabin.

"Corbett!" he roared. "By the craters of Luna, I couldn't contact you. Return to the *Polaris* on the double!"

"Is there something wrong, sir?" asked Tom, apprehensive after seeing the wildness of the jungle below him.

"Wrong?" blared Connel. "News from Earth—from the Academy! Roger's been cleared of all charges."

"Cleared?" stammered Tom.

"Absolutely! When I sealed the radar bridge after the crash, a security officer examined the settings on the scanners and transmitting equipment. They showed that Roger *had* been on duty at the time—that he had been tracking the ship as he claimed."

"Then what was the reason for the crash?"

"Security isn't sure yet. An acceleration control lever is missing from the wreckage. And it wasn't broken off as a result of the crash. Now Loring and Mason are wanted for further questioning."

Tom looked at his unit-mate, Astro. The big Venusian had his head turned to one side; he seemed to be staring out over the vast writhing jungle.

"Astro, did you hear?" asked Tom softly.

"Yeah," mumbled Astro in a small, choked voice. "Just don't ask me to turn around."

CHAPTER 12

How much longer before we reach the atmosphere of Tara, Manning?" asked Loring.

Roger bent over the chart table and quickly measured the distance between his present position and that of Tara.

"About two hours," he said, straightening up.

"Good!" said Loring. "Let me know soon as we get close."

"O.K.," replied the cadet.

"Hey, radar deck!" Mason's voice came over the intercom from the power deck of the *Space Devil*. "Don't forget to let me know when I have to cut down on thrust!"

"Take it easy, spaceboy," snapped Roger. "You'll know in plenty of time!" He turned back to the radar scanner and continued the never-ending sweep of space ahead.

After a week of checking and reconditioning the *Space Devil* in the wild Venusian jungles, Roger had become more and more disgusted with himself. Being a wanted spaceman had had its disadvantages on Spaceman's Row, but working in the steaming jungles, fighting deadly reptiles and insects, with Loring and Mason on his neck every minute had soured his appetite for adventure. Several times, when Roger had suggested a certain part be replaced, Loring and he had argued violently, and Roger had threatened to quit. Now, after the long tedious trip through space, Roger's relationship with the others was more strained than ever. The sure dependability of Tom on the control deck and Astro on the power deck made the work of Loring and Mason sloppy by comparison. Once, when Roger had been on radar watch, while the ship roared through the asteroid belt, collision with a small asteroid had threatened. Roger ordered a course change, but Mason, who had taken over the power deck, had been asleep. Luckily, Shinny had been near by, had made the course change, and saved the ship. Seething with anger, Roger had gone to the power deck and given the shiftless spaceman a terrific beating.

Over and over, conflicts had arisen among them as they blasted through deep space, and always, it seemed to Roger, he was in the middle of it. The only satisfaction he could find in the hazardous venture was the prospect of the five million credits. And even this had lost its excitement in the last few days, as his nerves stretched to the breaking point. Only the sly humor of Shinny had saved Roger from the monotony of the long haul through space.

Roger absently flipped the scanner to its farthest range. He had been observing the planet Tara for several hours and knew its shape fairly well. But he suddenly jerked to attention. His hands trembled slightly as he peered intently at the scope. Finally he slumped back. There was no doubt about it. On the scanner was a jet boat in flight.

"Hey, Loring! Shinny! Mason! Get up here on the double!" he yelled into the intercom.

"What's up?" demanded Loring.

"Get up here!" shouted Roger. "We're in for trouble—plenty of trouble!"

Presently the three spacemen were grouped around the scanner, staring at the unmistakable outline of a jet boat.

"By the rings of Saturn," declared Loring, "it must be Connel and his crew!"

"What're we going to do?" whined Mason.

Loring's face darkened. "Only one thing we can do now," he growled.

"What do you mean?" asked Roger.

"I mean that we're going to blast them!" Loring snarled. "Connel and whoever else is with him!"

"But—but—" stammered Roger, "the *Polaris* crew is down there!"

"Listen, Manning!" Loring turned to the cadet. "Have you forgotten that you're wanted by the Solar Guard? You give that bunch down there a chance and they'll make you a space crawler on prison rock!"

"Why—I—" stammered Roger. He knew what Loring had said was the truth. If it was Connel, there would be no question what would happen to him. He faced Loring. "What will you do to them?"

"One well-placed reactant bomb, and they'll never know a thing!" sneered Loring.

"But you don't have any bombs aboard," said Roger.

"A little of the fuel and I can build one easily enough," replied Loring. He turned to Mason. "Go below and suit up to go into the reaction chamber," he ordered. "Get an extra lead suit out. I'll go in and help you. And find something we can use for a trigger and a fuse." He smiled at Roger. "It might be a little crude, but it'll be fancy enough for what we want. I'm going to blast the *Polaris* from here back to your sweet little Space Academy!"

Mason and Loring left the radar bridge while Shinny and Roger watched the white blip of the jet boat.

"That could be Tom and Astro in that jet boat," said Roger softly to himself.

"I guess I'd better stand by the power deck while we maneuver," said Shinny. "We wanta stay hidden until Loring and Mason get that thing ready."

Roger nodded, and Shinny disappeared.

Maneuvering cautiously, Roger brought the *Space Devil* around to the night side of Tara opposite to the landing site of the *Polaris*.

Four hours later Loring and Mason came out of the reactant chamber carrying a small lead box. They placed it gently on the deck and began taking off their lead suits. Roger and Shinny stared at the box.

"There she is," said Loring. "Not much to look at, but there's enough juice in there to blast the *Polaris* into space junk!"

"Wait a minute, Loring!" said Roger. "There'll be no killing! No one gets hurt!"

"Got a squeamish stomach, eh, kid?" Loring laughed. He slapped Mason on the back. "Our little Space Cadet is suddenly worrying about his friends. The same friends that wanted to send him away to the prison asteroid."

"Blast the ship if you want," said Roger coldly, "but don't hurt the crew!"

"Listen, Manning!" snarled Loring. "If the crew gets hurt it ain't my fault. If they're in the ship, that's tough. If not, then that's O.K. with me. I ain't sending them any letter telling them I'm going to blast their ship and then have them come up after me with a space torpedo!"

Roger didn't answer. He turned away and climbed back to the radar bridge.

Loring followed him up the ladder.

"Don't get any ideas about warning your buddies, Manning, 'cause if you do, I'll blast you before I blast them!"

"Don't worry," replied Roger. "It's daytime on the other side of Tara now, where the *Polaris* is. The crew might be out on a scouting mission or making observations away from the ship. There's less chance of their being on the ship. If we're going to do it, let's get it over with!"

"O.K. with me," said Loring. "Take this wagon up toward Alpha Centauri a little way. Coming out of the sun, they won't see us. We'll use one of the jet boats to deliver our little present. I'll set the fuse, put the jet boat on automatic, and aim it right for the *Polaris*."

"All right," agreed Manning reluctantly. He turned to the chart table, plotted a course, and issued orders to Shinny at the controls and to Mason on the power deck. Soon the *Space Devil* was blasting away from the night side of the planet, heading toward the sun. When they reached an altitude of a thousand miles above the surface of the planet, Loring maneuvered the jet boat into position outside the ship and placed the crude reactant bomb inside. Ready, he gave Roger the signal to make the run out of the sun toward the *Polaris*. Roger relayed the orders to Shinny and Mason, and the *Space Devil* rocketed back toward the planet again.

Loring, sitting inside the jet boat, waited until they had reached an altitude of five hundred miles.

"All right, Manning," said Loring, "give me the course!"

Roger calculated the rotational speed of the planet, the *Space Devil's* altitude, and the speed of the jet boat. He drew a line between the *Space Devil* and *Polaris*, checked it on the astro compass, and reached for the intercom mike. He ran a dry tongue over his lips and called out the course.

"Course is one forty-three—" He caught himself and stared at the chart. Suppose Tom or Astro or anyone was near the ship? Even if he missed by several hundred yards, the bomb would certainly be fatal. If he only changed the course one degree, at a range of five hundred miles, it would miss the *Polaris* by several miles. And Loring wouldn't be able to see anything because of the dust cloud.

"Course corrected," said Roger. "New course is one forty-two!"

"One forty-two!" repeated Loring.

Roger sat back and waited for the small space craft to blast off from the ship. In his mind, he saw Loring setting the trigger on the bomb, adjusting the controls, setting the automatic pilot, and then pressing the acceleration button. Roger gripped the sides of the chart table and stared at the radar scanner. A fast-moving blip was streaking across its surface. Loring had started the jet boat.

His eyes showing his great fear, Roger watched the blip as it sped down like a maddened hornet toward the *Polaris* resting on its directional fins in the green jungle. He could hear the hatch slam closed below as Loring re-entered the ship, but he continued to watch the rapidly moving blip.

Suddenly it disappeared, and Roger knew it had reached Tara. He slumped back in his chair. His eyes were glassy, his ears deaf to the roar of triumph from below as Loring and Mason, watching the flight of the jet boat on the control deck teleceiver screen, saw it explode. Roger couldn't move. He had fired a reactant bomb at Tom and Astro.

"By the craters of Luna," roared Connel, "we've been attacked!"

The four Earthmen, exploring a valley several miles north of the *Polaris*, had been thrown to the ground when the bomb landed. Connel's reaction was immediate and decisive.

"Get into the jet boat! All of you! We've got to get back to the *Polaris*! If our ship is smashed, we'll spend the rest of our lives fighting this jungle!"

In a matter of seconds the four spacemen were rocketing over the jungle toward the *Polaris*. Presently they came to an enormous dust cloud that had mushroomed out over the trees. It was so thick Tom found it difficult to pilot the small craft.

"Any danger of radioactivity in this dust, sir?" asked Astro.

"Always that possibility, Astro," answered Connel. "We'll know soon enough!" He flipped on a built-in Geiger counter on the dashboard of the jet boat, and immediately the cabin was filled with a loud ticking that warned of danger.

"The count is up to seven fifty, sir," said Astro. "Not enough to bother you unless you're in it a long time."

"There's the *Polaris*, sir," yelled Tom. "She's still on her directional fins! They missed her! She's O.K.!"

"By the blessed rings of Saturn, she is!" exclaimed Connel. "Go on, Tom, give this baby the gun! If we have to die, let's die like spacemen, in space, fighting with spaceman's weapons, not crawling around here in the jungle like worms!"

The three boys smiled at their skipper's rousing statement. "This is the time," thought Tom, "when I'd rather have Major Connel in command than anyone else in the Solar Guard." If there was to be a fight, then they certainly had found the man who knew how to do just that! Fight!

Tom swooped over the treetops recklessly, and fearing the blast had damaged the jet-boat air lock, brought the small craft to rest in the blinding dust a few yards away from the *Polaris*.

Three minutes later the four spacemen had separated and were standing by their respective posts. Hasty but thorough checks were made to determine the damage, and finding none, they prepared to raise ship.

"All clear forward and up," Alfie reported in a high squeaking voice.

"Energize the cooling pumps," shouted Tom.

Astro had already started the mighty pumps, their vibrations rocking the ship, and Tom began counting the seconds.

"Stand by to raise ship. Minus five—four—three—two—one—*zeeroooooo!*"

Paying scant attention to the crush of sudden acceleration, Tom gave the ship all the power she could take for the climb out of Tara's atmosphere, and soon they were rocketing through the airless void of space. Alfie and Connel hurriedly swept the area with the radar scanner for the attacking intruder.

"There she is!" roared Connel. "There!" He placed a finger on a white blip on the scanner. "By the craters of Luna, that's an Earth ship!" The fear of an outer-space invasion by hostile people from another world had been in the back of his mind, but he had been reluctant to voice his fears in front of the cadets. "And she's an old one at that!" he exclaimed. "Not even armed. I know that class vessel. Corbett!" he shouted.

"Aye, aye, sir," replied Tom.

"Put the ship on automatic flight, attack-approach pattern number three. Then stand by to send a message to whoever's manning that ship!"

"Aye, aye, sir!" replied Tom. He hurriedly set the delicate device that would fly the ship in a preplanned course of zigzag maneuvers and opened the circuits of the teleceivers.

"All set for the message, sir," reported Tom.

"Tell them," said Connel heavily, his voice cold, "whoever they are, that I'll give them two minutes to surrender. If they don't, I'll blast them into protons!"

"Very well, sir," said Tom. He turned to the teleceiver and began twirling the dials.

"Attention! Attention! Rocket cruiser *Polaris* to spaceship X. *Polaris* to spaceship X. You are ordered to surrender within two minutes or we will attack. By order of Major Connel, Senior Line Officer, Solar Guard."

He switched the teleceiver for reception and waited. In a moment the screen blurred and then an image appeared. Tom gasped. It was Roger!

"Tom, Tom," yelled Roger. "Tom, this is me—Roger!"

"Roger! What're you doing out here? How'd you get here?"

"I can't explain now," said Roger. "I—I—"

Tom interrupted him. "Roger, you've been cleared! The investigation of the crash on the station proved that Loring and Mason are guilty. They're wanted for the crash and the deaths of Jardine and Bangs!"

"What! You mean—" stammered Roger.

"Yes. Loring and Mason did the whole thing!" supplied Tom.

"Look, Tom," pleaded Roger, "give me ten minutes. Don't fire for ten minutes! I'm going to try an idea. If I'm not successful, then open up and blast us back to Mars!"

"Roger, wait!" shouted Tom. "What's going on? What're you doing on that ship?"

"I can't talk now," answered Roger. "Loring and Mason are on the ship with me. Remember—ten minutes—and if I don't contact you, then open fire!"

CHAPTER 13

Roger flipped off the teleceiver. He stared at the darkened screen and began estimating the chances of success for a plan he had in mind. Deciding that, regardless of what happened, he had to take over the ship, he got up and turned toward the hatch and the gun locker. He stopped cold. Loring stood framed in the doorway, a paralo-ray gun in each hand.

"Just stand right where you are, spaceboy!" snapped Loring. "You want ten minutes, huh? Ten minutes for what? I thought there was something funny going on when we missed the *Polaris* with that bomb!"

"You knew all along I didn't have anything to do with that crash back on the station, didn't you?" shouted Roger. His eyes blazed angrily.

"Yeah. So what?" growled Loring. "Hey, Mason," he yelled over his shoulder, "get up here in a hurry! We gotta work fast!"

"What are you going to do?" asked Roger.

"You're still valuable to us, Manning," said Loring with a crooked grin. "You're going to ensure our getting what we came after!"

Mason stepped through the door. "Yeah, Loring?"

Loring quickly told him of Roger's attempt to work with Connel.

"Take our spaceboy down below and lock him in a storage compartment." He handed over one of the paralo-ray guns, and Mason shoved the muzzle into Roger's stomach.

"Get moving, Manning!" he snarled. "I'd like nothing better than to let you have it right now!"

Roger smiled, knowing Mason still harbored a grudge for the beating he had taken earlier on the trip.

"When you have him locked up, get back on the control deck," said Loring.

"We're going to do some old-fashioned bargaining with 'Blast-off' Connel!"

"Bargaining?" exclaimed Roger.

"Yeah! One slightly used Space Cadet for what we came after—the copper satellite!"

"Connel won't bargain," said Roger. "Not for me, not for anything. You don't know him!"

"I know this, Manning!" said Loring. "I'm going to get on the teleceiver and tell Connel that if he doesn't blast away from here *right now*, you're a dead Space Cadet!" He jerked his head toward the door. "All right, take him below and tell Shinny to stand by on the power deck. In case Connel won't bargain, we'll have to make a run for it!"

"Right," said Mason as he shoved the paralo-ray gun deeper into Roger's stomach. "Move, Manning!"

Roger climbed down the ladder and through the long passageway of the *Space Devil*. He passed Shinny on the way down.

"What's going on here?" demanded Shinny, seeing Mason with the paralo-ray gun.

"We missed with the bomb," said Mason, "and Connel raised ship. He's ready to blast us if we don't surrender right away. Loring's trying to make a deal with him."

"What kind of a deal?" asked Shinny.

"Hot-shot Manning for the satellite!"

"He hasn't told you everything, Mr. Shinny," said Roger in his casual drawl. "They are the ones who caused the crash of the *Annie Jones* and the deaths of Jardine and Bangs. They framed me!"

"Then," mused Shinny, "you're cleared?"

"Yeah," growled Mason, "he's cleared! Cleared for a long swim in space if Connel doesn't do what Loring tells him! Get in there!" Mason shoved Roger into the cramped storage compartment. He locked the door and turned to Shinny.

"Loring wants you to stand by the power deck in case Connel won't play ball. We might have to make a run for it."

"Yeah, yeah," said Shinny, "I'll stand by the power deck."

Mason turned and walked away. Shinny followed him, a curious gleam in his eyes. Up on the control deck, Loring was twisting the dials in front of the teleceiver screen.

"*Space Devil* to *Polaris*—*Space Devil* to *Polaris*—come in, *Polaris*." He twisted another dial and watched the darkened screen anxiously. After a moment the screen blurred, and Tom's face gradually came into sharp focus.

"Loring!" gasped Tom. "Where's Roger?"

"Never mind him, you punk!" snarled Loring. "Tell that fatheaded Connel I wanta talk to him! Make it fast!"

Tom's face disappeared to be replaced by the raging features of Major Connel. "You murdering space rat!" he roared. "I've given you two minutes to surrender and, by the craters of Luna, you've only got thirty seconds left!"

"It'll only take ten seconds to tell you that if you don't get outta here Cadet Manning gets blasted!"

"What?" roared Connel.

"That's right," snarled Loring. "You're the one that's got thirty seconds to get out of here, or Manning takes a swim in space!"

"Why, you—" Connel's face was twisted with rage. "You can't threaten me!"

"I ain't threatening you," said Loring, "*I'm telling you!* If you don't get started, you'll never see Manning again. Or if you do, you won't recognize him! Now make up your mind, Connel!"

The Solar Guard officer hesitated. "Give me two minutes," he said, "and I'll call you back. Two minutes."

"Two minutes," repeated Loring, "and if I don't hear from you by then, or if you try any funny stuff, Manning gets it!"

Aboard the *Polaris*, the screen darkened, and Connel, his fists clenched, turned to Tom.

"We're helpless, Tom," he said softly. "Now that we have proof of Roger's innocence, I have to do everything in my power to save him."

Tom didn't say anything. Suddenly Connel smashed one huge fist into another. "But by the blessed rings of Saturn, when I *do* get my hands on that Loring, I'll—I'll—" He broke off suddenly and turned back to the teleceiver. "I'm going to do what he wants, Tom. Roger's life is worth a dozen like Loring, and we'll have to take a chance that Loring will keep his word. After all," continued the big officer softly, "our mission is complete. We've tested the transmitter and found it to be more than we expected. No real reason why we should stay around here any longer."

"Yes, sir," stammered Tom. "Sir, I—I—"

Connel waved him silent with his hand. "You don't need to say anything, Tom. It's just one of those things. Still I can't help wondering what they came out here for." He turned to the dials on the teleceiver and began twisting them. "I'll call him, and you stand by to blast out of here."

Nicholas Shinny sat on the power deck and listened to Loring issue orders over the intercom.

"I don't know if Connel will go for it, or not," said Loring, "but just in case he doesn't, we gotta get outta here fast! You got that, Shinny?"

"Yeah," answered Shinny, "I got it!"

"Mason," yelled Loring, "you take over on the radar bridge!"

"All ready up here," said Mason.

"Well, be sure we've got a clear trajectory out. Better take us into the sun Alpha Centauri. That way, maybe they'll miss us on their radar. The sun will show all sorts of blips on their screen."

"O.K.," said Mason. "You think he'll go for it?"

"I don't know," answered Loring, "but if he doesn't, it's going to be space dust for Manning."

Shinny got up and walked around the deserted power deck. His legs felt weak. The plan he had made was a desperate one. Over and over, he checked the operation in his mind. It would have to be quick, sure, and sudden. That was the only thing that would ensure success. "Yes, sir," he thought, "if we can surprise 'em, we can get away with it." He dug out a piece of chewing tobacco, took a bite, eyed the remaining piece, and then shoved the whole thing in his mouth. His cheek bulged.

He went to the intercom and flipped it on. "Hey, Loring," he yelled. "I've got to check the timer on number-three rocket. She's not acting just right. It'll take me about a minute."

"O.K.," came Loring's reply, "but make it snappy."

The timers were to the left of the control board, but Shinny turned to the right and the ladder leading to the lower deck. He eased the hatch open, glanced around, and then climbed down quickly. He stopped at a locker, opened the doors quietly, and took out two paralo-ray guns and two rifles. Then, closing the doors, he made his way to the opposite side of the ship.

"Hey, Manning!" he whispered through the closed storeroom hatch. "Can ya hear me?"

"Who is it?" asked Roger.

"Me—Shinny," hissed the wizened spaceman. He opened the hatch and Roger quickly stepped out.

"What's the idea?" gasped Roger when Shinny shoved a rifle and pistol into his hands.

"I ain't got time to explain now," said Shinny. "We've got to hurry if we're going to take over this tub."

Roger's eyes glowed. "You mean—"

"Never mind what I mean," said Shinny. "Just listen. Loring's on the control deck and Mason's on the radar bridge. Loring's just talked to Connel. He's trying to make him blast outta here. If Connel doesn't, Loring's going to dump you in space!"

"Yeah, I know. That murdering space crawler!" snarled Roger. He gripped the rifle tightly. "I'll blast him—"

"Now wait a minute," hissed Shinny. "You go up and get Loring, see? Make it look like you got out by yourself. If you can handle him, O.K. I'll stay in back, and if anything goes wrong, I'll back you up!"

"Fine," said Roger. He patted the spaceman on the back and smiled. "Don't worry, Mr. Shinny, nothing will go wrong!"

"Watch your step. That Loring is a smart cookie!"

Roger turned into the passageway and made his way silently to the control-deck hatch. He peered around the edge of the hatch and saw Loring sitting in front of the televiewer screen, his back toward Roger. The cadet quickly stepped into the control room, leveled the rifle, and said quietly, "All right, Loring, keep your hands in view!"

Loring spun around and stared openmouthed at Roger. "Mann—" he gasped.

"Yeah, me!" said Roger. "Call Mason and tell him to come down here on the double. But one wrong move, Loring, and I'll give you a quick freeze with this ray gun!"

Moving slowly, Loring turned to the intercom and flipped the switch. "Hey, Mason," he yelled. "Come down here a minute, will ya?"

"What do you want?" growled Mason. "I've got to figure out this course."

Roger stepped close to Loring, raising the gun.

Loring licked his lips and turned back to the intercom. "Don't gimme any back talk! I said get down here!"

Suddenly the teleceiver came to life. "*Polaris* to *Space Devil*! Come in, Loring! This is Major Connel on the *Polaris* calling Loring on the *Space Devil*!"

The suddenness of the voice startled Roger, and for a split second he took his eyes off Loring. In that instant Loring leaped for the boy, grabbing at the rifle. The quickness of his lunge caught Roger off guard and he was thrown back against the bulkhead, but he held onto the rifle as Loring tried to twist it out of his grasp.

"What th—" cried Mason from the ladder leading to the radar bridge. When he saw Roger and Loring struggling, he grabbed for the paralo-ray gun at his side. Just at that moment Shinny stepped through the hatch and fired his rifle. Mason was frozen into a rigid statue, unable to move.

"All right, Loring," yelled Shinny, "step back or I'll blast you like I did Mason!"

Roger wrenched the rifle out of Loring's grasp and stepped back. "Good work, Mr. Shinny!" he said to the little spaceman. "You sure figured it right!"

"Attention! Attention! This is Connel on the *Polaris*. Come in, Loring ..."

Shinny looked over at Roger and winked. "Better answer him, while I get this joker locked up." He motioned to Loring who stood backed up against the bulkhead, his hands high over his head.

"You dirty double-crossing space rat!" he snarled at Shinny.

"Now, now, none of that," said Shinny, leveling the rifle. "If you get too noisy, I'll freeze you like I did Mason to keep your trap shut!"

Loring cast a sidelong glance at Mason, who stood as if carved out of marble. The effects of the ray blast were devastating, having paralyzed his entire nervous system. While the victim was still able to breathe and his heartbeat remained normal, he was unable to move so much as an eyelid. The gun was developed after all lethal weapons had been outlawed by the Solar Alliance. Though any victim could be released from its paralyzing effect by a neutralizing charge from the same gun, while under its power the victim was reduced to a state of mild hysteria. He was able to hear, see, and think, but not to act. When released, it was not unusual to see a man crumple to the floor from exhaustion.

Mason was frozen into a rigid statue, unable to move

Loring marched meekly in front of Shinny to the storage room that had held Roger. The cadet spaceman remained on the control deck. He twisted the dials of the teleceiver and spoke into the mike.

"*Space Devil* to Major Connel. Come in! This is Manning on the *Space Devil* calling Major Connel ..."

"Manning!" shouted Connel. "I thought you were a prisoner!"

"Ah, it was nothing, skipper," said Roger blandly. "I just took over the ship—with a little help, of course!"

"A little help?" asked Connel. "From whom?"

Roger then gave the officer a complete review of what had happened to him since leaving the space station, finishing with Shinny's aid in his escape.

"Why would he want to help you?" asked Connel.

"I don't know, sir," replied Roger.

"Well, never mind," said Connel. "I suppose you two can handle that ship all right between you. Land on Tara as soon as you can. I'll get the details then!"

"Aye, aye, sir," replied Roger. Then, just before breaking contact, he yelled into the mike, "Hey, Astro—Tom! See ya in a few minutes!"

As the teleceiver screen darkened, Shinny reappeared. He had released Mason from the effects of the ray charge, and both Mason and Loring were safe in the storage room. He walked over and slapped Roger on the back.

"Well, it looks like we did it, sonny boy!" he said.

Roger turned to look at the wizened spaceman who still was chewing on the plug of tobacco. "What made you do this for me, Mr. Shinny?" asked Roger quietly.

"Tell ya a little secret," said Shinny, with a merry twinkle in his eye. "I was in the Solar Guard for twenty years. Enlisted man. Got into an accident and hurt my leg, but it wasn't in the line of duty, so I was tossed out without a pension. Ever since then I been kinda bitter, you might say. And, strangely enough, it was Major Connel that kicked me out."

"But you—you—" gasped Roger.

"Let's just say," said Shinny with a smile, "that once you're a Solar Guardsman, you're always a Guardsman. Now, how about getting this wagon down to Tara?"

"Yeah, yeah, sure," said Roger absently, his eyes trailing after the small limping figure. Once a Solar Guardsman, always a Guardsman, he thought. Smiling, he turned to the control board. He felt the same way. He was a Guardsman, and it was good to be back home!

CHAPTER 14

Major Connel paced nervously in front of the group of spacemen. Tom, Roger, Astro, Alfie, and Mr. Shinny were lounging around the small clearing between the *Polaris* and the *Space Devil*. A piece of thin space cloth had been stretched between the two ships to shield the men from the blazing sun. Connel stopped in front of Roger and Shinny.

"And you say the satellite is three-quarters solid copper?" asked Connel.

"Yes, sir," replied Roger, "at least that's what Loring and Mason told us."

"Where is it?" asked Connel. "I mean, where exactly?"

"I spotted her coming in, sir," replied Roger. "I'd say she was about three hundred thousand miles outside of Tara in perfect orbit."

"By the blessed rings of Saturn," exclaimed Connel, "it's almost too good to be true! The whole Solar Alliance needs copper desperately. And if what you say is true, that's enough to last for a hundred and fifty years!"

"Didn't you have any idea they discovered it, sir?" asked Tom. "I mean, when they took that unauthorized flight on your first trip out here?"

"Didn't suspect a thing, Tom," replied Connel. "I thought they had gotten a little space rocky on some homemade rocket juice and just went on a wingding. Imagine the colossal nerve of those two wanting to corner the market with the largest deposit of copper ever found."

"How do you plan to get it back, Major?" asked Shinny.

"I don't know, Shinny—"

"*Mr.* Shinny!" snapped the wizened spaceman. "*I'm* not one of your cadets!"

"Still the hotheaded rocket buster, eh?" asked Connel, eying the toothless spaceman. "It was the same thing that got you kicked out of the Solar Guard twenty years ago!"

"Wasn't either! And you know it!" snapped Shinny. "You retired me because I busted my leg!"

"That helped," said Connel, "but the main reason was because you were too hotheaded. Couldn't take orders!"

"Well," said Shinny doggedly, "I ain't in no Solar Guard now, and when you talk to me, it's *Mr.* Shinny!"

"Why, you old goat!" exploded Connel. "I ought to arrest you for aiding criminals!"

"You can't do a thing to me," barked Shinny. "Prospecting is prospecting, whether it's in the asteroid belt or out here on Tara!"

Unable to hold back any longer, the four space cadets suddenly roared with laughter at the sight of the two old space foes jawing at each other. Actually, Connel and Shinny were glad to see each other. And when they saw the boys doubled up with laughter, they couldn't help laughing also. Finally Connel turned to Roger.

"Can you find that satellite again?" he asked.

"Yes, sir!" Roger grinned.

"All right, then," said Connel finally, "let's go take a look at it. I still won't believe it until I see it!"

"Who's hardheaded now?" snorted Shinny, climbing into the *Polaris*.

Later, as the rocket cruiser blasted smoothly through space, Connel joined Roger and Alfie on the radar deck. The two cadets were bent over the radar scanner.

"Pick her up yet?" asked Connel.

"There she is, right there, sir," said Roger, placing a finger on a circular white blip on the scanner. "But the magnascope shows pretty rugged country. I think we'd better take a look on the opposite side. Maybe we can find a better place to touch down."

"Very well, Manning," replied Connel. "Do what you think best. Tell Tom to land as soon as possible."

"Aye, aye, sir," replied Roger.

Leaving Alfie on watch at the scanner, Roger hurried down the ladder to the control deck where Tom was seated in front of the great board.

"Tom," called Roger, walking up behind his unit-mate, "we're going to take a look at this baby on the other side. See if we can't find a better place to touch down.

Stand by to pick up the surface of the satellite on the teleceiver as soon as we get close enough."

"O.K., Roger," said Tom. "Where are you going?"

"Down to Loring and Mason in the cooler! I want to see their faces when I tell them they finally are getting where they wanted to go, but under slightly different circumstances!"

Tom laughed and turned back to the board. "Power deck, check in!"

"Power deck, aye," replied Astro. "When do we set down on the precious rock, Tom?" asked the Venusian.

"Should be soon, Astro," said Tom. "Better stand by for maneuvering."

"Right!" replied Astro.

Tom turned his full attention to the control board and the teleceiver screen above his head. He was happier than he had ever been in his life. The report sent back to Space Academy by Major Connel had been answered with a commendation to both Roger and Shinny for capturing Loring and Mason. With Roger back in the unit, Tom was at peace. Even Alfie was overjoyed at seeing Roger back aboard the *Polaris*.

And Tom had noticed that Major Connel was beginning to call them by their first names!

"Radar deck to control deck!" said Alfie. "From casual observations, Tom, the surface of the far side of the satellite is more suitable for a touchdown. I would suggest you observe the planetoid yourself with the magnascope and draw your own conclusions."

"O.K.," replied Tom. He switched the teleceiver screen on to the more powerful magnascope and studied the surface of the small celestial body. He saw a deep valley with a flat hard surface set between two tall cliffs. It would be a tricky spot for a landing, but it looked like the best place available. Tom snapped open the intercom.

"Attention! Attention! Stand by for touchdown. Power deck stand by for deceleration. Radar bridge stand by for range and altitude checks!" Sharply, crisply, Tom's orders crackled through the ship.

Working together with the ease and thoroughness of men well acquainted with their jobs, Astro and Shinny on the power deck, Roger and Alfie on the radar bridge, and Tom on the control deck handling the delicate maneuvering, combined to bring the great ship to a safe landing on the dry valley floor of the satellite.

"Touchdown!" yelled Tom and began securing the ship. Two minutes later the entire crew faced Major Connel for briefing.

"We'll all go out to different parts of the satellite and make geological tests," announced Connel. "We'll pair off, two to a jet boat. Astro and Roger, Alfie and Mr. Shinny, Tom and myself. This is a simple test." He held up a delicate instrument and a vial full of colorless liquid. "You simply pour a little of this liquid, about a spoonful, on the ground, wait about five minutes, and then stick the end of this into the spot where you poured the liquid." He held up a two-foot steel shaft a quarter inch in diameter, fastened to a clock-face gauge with numbers from one to a thousand. The other end of the shaft was needle sharp. "When you stick this into the ground, there'll be a reading on the meter. Relay it to me. This way well get an estimate of the amount of copper in a three-mile area for a depth of a hundred feet. It must be more than two hundred tons per square mile to make it worth while!"

He held up the testing equipment for all to see and explained its use once more. Then, giving each team a kit, he ordered them to the jet boats.

Just before the crew of Earthmen left the *Polaris*, Connel gave them last-minute instructions.

"Report back to the *Polaris* in one hour. Make as many tests as you can over as wide an area as possible. Don't forget to leave one man in the jet boat while the other is making the test. Keep your audio communicator in the jet boat on at all times. And be sure your belt communicator is always open. Check your oxygen supply and space suits. All clear?"

One by one, the spacemen checked in through the audio communicators that all was clear. The sliding hatch on the side of the *Polaris* was opened, and the jet boats blasted out into the brilliant sunlight of Alpha Centauri, going in three different directions.

Tom piloted his small craft over the rugged surface of the satellite, circling the larger peaks and swooping into the small valleys. Connel would indicate when it was time to stop, and Tom would set the craft down. While Connel made the tests, Tom would talk to the others over the audio communicators. The three small ships covered the satellite quickly in evenly divided sections, reporting their readings on the needlelike instrument to Connel, who kept recording the reports on a pad at his knee.

An hour later the boats returned to the *Polaris* and the Earthmen assembled in the control room. Connel, Tom, and Alfie were busy reducing the readings of the tests into recognizable copper ton estimates per square mile.

Finally Connel turned around, wiped his brow, and faced the others.

"This is one of the greatest discoveries for Earthmen since they learned how to blast off!" The big officer paused and then held up the results of the tests. "This satellite is *really* three-quarters solid copper!"

There was a loud mumble as everyone began talking at once.

"How are we going to get it back home, sir?" asked Tom. "Wouldn't hauling it back in spaceships cost too much?"

"Yes, it would, Corbett," answered Connel, "but I've got an idea how we can lick that problem."

"Can't see how you can lick it," snorted Shinny, "unless you take the whole blasted satellite back!"

"That's exactly what I'm going to do!" answered Connel.

"What?" exclaimed Roger, momentarily forgetting he was addressing a senior officer. "How in blazes are you going to do that?"

Connel turned to the chart-screen projector and switched it on. Immediately an image of Earth and its Moon, and much farther away the sun, was visible. Connel stepped to the screen and pointed to Moon.

"The Moon is a captive satellite of Earth, revolving around Earth the same way Earth revolves around the sun. It's the same situation we have here. This satellite is a captive of Tara, and Tara is a captive of Alpha Centauri. The difference is that the satellite is a peanut compared in size to the Moon, being only about fifteen miles in diameter. I'm not sure, but I think I can get enough reactant energy out of the *Space Devil's* fuel supply to blast the satellite out of Tara's grip and send it back to our solar system in one piece!"

"You mean, sir," asked Tom, perplexed, "you'll tear the satellite out of Tara's gravitational pull?"

"That's right, Tom," replied Connel, "using the same principle to clear gravity that we use on the *Polaris* or any spaceship. Enough power from the rockets will blast the **Polaris** off Tara. Well, if you can get enough power, you can blast this satellite out of Tara's grip also, since the only thing holding it here is the gravity of Tara—the same thing that holds the Moon in orbit around Earth!"

Astro's eyes bulged. He looked at Connel blankly. "Why, sir," he stammered, "it'd take—take—a ***ton*** of reactant fuel to pull something that size away from Tara. The **Polaris** is a kiddy car in comparison!"

"You're right, Astro," said Connel, "but there's one thing you've forgotten. The copper of the satellite itself. That's going to be the main source of power. The reactant fuel from the **Space Devil** will serve only as a starter, a trigger, you might say, to make use of the copper as fuel!"

Once again Astro gasped. "Then—then—there isn't anything to stop you, sir," he finished slowly.

Connel smiled. "I know there isn't. I'm going to contact Space Academy now for permission to pitch the biggest ball in the history of man!"

CHAPTER 15

Well, I'll be a star-gazing lunatic!" exclaimed Roger a few minutes later. "You really think that you can blast this satellite out of its orbit?"

"Not only that, Manning," said Connel with a smile, "but I might be able to get it back to our sun faster than we could get back ourselves."

"Why that would be the biggest project ever attempted by man, sir," said Tom. "You'd be transporting an entire satellite from one star system to another!"

"That's right, Corbett," said Connel. "I've just finished talking to Space Academy and they've given me permission to do anything I think necessary to accomplish just that. Now pay close attention to me, all of you. We haven't much time."

Tom, Roger, Astro, Alfie, and Mr. Shinny gathered in a close circle around the major on the control deck of the *Polaris* and watched him as he drew several rough diagrams on a piece of paper.

"Getting the satellite back is the trickiest part of the whole operation. Astro, are you sure you made a correct estimate on the amount of reactant fuel in the *Space Devil*?"

"Yes, sir," replied Astro. "I checked it four times, and Mr. Shinny checked it, too!"

"All right, then, listen," said Connel. "I've given the satellite a name. From now on we call it Junior. And this will be known as Junior's Pitch! I've explained how Junior is a captive satellite revolving around Tara, the same way our Moon revolves around Earth. We have two problems. One is to blast it out of Tara's grip. And the other is to take advantage of Tara's orbital speed around its sun Alpha Centauri, *and* Junior's orbital speed around Tara. We've got to combine the velocities of the orbits, so that when we do spring Junior loose, he'll gain in speed!"

"But how do we get the orbital speeds to help us, Major?" asked Alfie. His glasses had slipped to the very end of his nose.

"If you'd give the major a chance, he'd tell you, Big Brain," drawled Roger. Alfie gave Roger a withering look and turned back to the major.

"Do you remember when you were kids and tied a rock on the end of a rope and then swung it around your head?" asked Connel.

"Sure, sorta like a slingshot," said Astro.

"That's right, Astro," said Connel, "and if you released the rope, the rock would fly in the direction it was headed, ***when you let go***!"

"I get it," cried Tom excitedly. "The gravity of Tara is the rope holding Junior—ah"—he fumbled—"making it swing around!"

"And the reactant power of the ***Space Devil*** placed in the right spot would be the trigger to make it let go!" commented Roger.

"It's as simple as that, boys!" said Connel with a smile.

"But how in the blazing beams of the sun are you going to ***stop*** that blasted thing when you get it rolling?" asked Shinny.

"The chances of Junior hitting anything on the way home are so small it doesn't present a problem. So we just aim Junior for our solar system! Later on, arrangements can be made to steer it into an orbit around our sun."

"You know," wheezed Shinny, his merry eyes twinkling, "that sounds pretty neat!"

"It is," replied Connel. He leaned against the control-board desk top and folded his arms across his massive chest. He looked at each of the cadets and Shinny a long time before speaking. Finally he stepped forward and stood among them, turning now and then to speak directly to each of them.

"We have only four days, five hours, and some few minutes to pull Junior out of Tara's grip, and later, the grip of Alpha Centauri. You boys will have to work as you've never worked before. You'll do things you never dreamed you could do. You'll work until your brains ache and your bodies scream. But when you're finished, you will have accomplished one of man's greatest challenges. You're going to do all this because I know you can—and I'm going to see that you do! Is that clear?"

There was a barely audible "Yes, sir" from the cadets.

"The six of us, working together, are going to send a hunk of copper fifteen miles in diameter hurtling through twenty-three million million miles of space, so let's get that ball rolling. ***Right now!***"

With Major Connel roaring, pleading, and blasting, four young cadets and a derelict spaceman began the monumental task of assembling the mass of information necessary for the satellite's big push through space. During the three days that their project had been under way, Tom, Roger, Astro, Alfie, and Mr. Shinny worked, as Major Connel promised, as they had never worked before.

Late in the afternoon of the third day Connel stepped through the hatch of the control deck where Tom was busy over a table of ratios for balancing the amount of thrust from each of the reactant-power units. The power units were to give Junior its initial thrust out of the gravity of Tara.

"Well, Corbett," asked Connel, "how're you making out with the ratios?"

"I've finished them, sir," replied Tom, looking up at the major. His face was drawn, his eyes red from lack of sleep. "But I just can't seem to get a time for escaping the orbit on a true tangent."

"Have you tried making an adjustment for the overall pull of both components?" asked Connel. "That of Tara and of Alpha Centauri on Junior?" He picked up the paper Tom had been working on and glanced over the figures.

"Yes, sir," replied Tom, "but I still can't seem to make it come out right!"

"You'll get it, Tom," said Connel. "Go over it again. But remember. Time's running out. Just one day and about twenty hours left." Connel's voice was friendly—more friendly than at any time Tom could remember. He smiled, and taking a fresh sheet of paper, he began the complicated calculations of escape time all over again.

Connel slipped out of the control room and went below to the power deck, where Astro and Mr. Shinny had been working without sleep for over fifty hours. When Connel slipped into the room he found the two men puzzling over a drawing board.

"What seems to be the trouble, Astro?" asked Connel.

Astro turned, startled. "We've tried building that lead baffle for the reactant units five times now, sir," said Astro. "We're having a hard time getting the correct amount of reactant power we need in a unit this small."

"Maybe you're trying to make it ***too*** small, Astro," commented Connel, looking over the drawing. "Remember, this unit has but one job. To **start** the reaction. When the reaction fuel gets hot enough, it'll start a reaction of the copper on Junior and sustain itself. Try a smaller amount of the reactant. But whatever you do, keep working. Only a day and a few hours left."

Connel looked at Shinny. "Keep him working, Mr. Shinny," he ordered. "I know he can do it. Just keep him going."

Shinny grinned and nodded.

"I'll try, sir," said Astro, shaking his head, "but I won't guarantee it—"

Connel cut him off with a roar. "Cadet Astro, I don't want your guarantee! *I want that unit. Now build it!*"

Hour after hour the cadets racked their brains for what seemed like impossible answers to an impossible task. Working until their eyes closed fast shut, they would lie down right where they were—power deck, control deck, or radar bridge—and sleep. They would awake, still groggy, drink hot tea, eat cold sandwiches, and continue their struggle with time and astrophysics.

One by one, the problems were solved and set aside for newer ones that arose on the way. Each cadet worked in his particular field, and all of their information was assembled and co-ordinated by Major Connel. More than once, Connel had found the clever minds of his cadets reaching for answers to questions he knew would have troubled the professors back at Space Academy. Connel, his eye on the clock, his sharp tongue lashing out when he thought he detected unclear thinking, raced from one department to another while the incessant work continued. On the morning of the fourth day he walked into the radar bridge where Roger and Alfie had been working steadily for seventy-two hours on an electronic fuse to trigger the reactant units.

"There you are, skipper," said Roger. "The fuse is all yours. Delivered twelve hours ahead of time!"

"Good work, Roger. You too, Alfie. Excellent!" said Connel, his eyes appraising the fuse.

"Ah, that's nothing, skipper," said Roger with a smile. "Anyone could have done it with Alfie here to help. He's got a brain like a calculator!"

"Now, I want to see how smart you two really are!" said Connel.

"Huh?" asked Roger stupidly. Alfie had slumped to the deck, holding his head in his hands.

"I want a communications unit," said Connel, "that can send out a constant beam, a signal Space Academy can pick up to follow Junior in transit back to Earth."

"In twelve hours?" exploded Roger. "Impossible, skipper!"

"*Cadet Manning*," roared Connel, "I don't want your *opinion*, I asked for that *unit*!"

"But one day, sir," said Roger. "Not even a day. Twelve hours. I can't, sir. I'm sorry. I'm so tired I can't see straight."

Alfie let out a low moan.

Connel studied the two cadets. He was aware that he had already asked them to do the impossible, and they had done it. And they deserved to be let alone. But Major Connel wasn't himself unless he had given every ounce of energy he had left, or the energy left in those around him. He patted Roger on the shoulder and spoke softly.

"Roger, did I ever tell you that I think you have one of the finest brains for electronics I've ever seen? And that Alfie is sure to have a brilliant future in astrophysics?"

Roger stammered. "Why—ah—thank you, sir—"

Alfie looked up at Connel and then struggled to his feet.

"You know, Roger," he said haltingly, "if we took that unit we came out here to test—you know, the transmitter unit—"

Roger cut him off. "Yeah, I was just thinking the same thing. We could borrow some of the reaction mass that Astro got out of the *Space Devil* and use that as a power source."

Connel backed away from the two cadets and tiptoed off the bridge. He smiled to himself. He was going to win his race with time yet! And he was going to do it because he had learned long before that you could only push a man so far, then you had to sit down, pat him on the back, tell him how smart he was, and he would push himself. Connel almost laughed out loud.

Six hours later Connel sat in his quarters puzzling over one of the many minor problems of Junior's Pitch when he heard footsteps behind him. He turned. Astro, Tom, Roger, Alfie, and Shinny walked silently into the room. Connel stared.

"Wha—what is it?" he demanded.

"We're finished, sir," said Tom simply.

"Finished?" exploded Connel. "You mean—"

"That's what he means, skipper," said Shinny. His eyes were bloodshot for want of sleep, but there was a merry twinkle left tugging at the corners.

"Everything?" asked Connel.

"Everything, sir," said Roger. "The power units are built and the fuses installed. All it needs is to be set. Tom's worked out the ratios and the amount of reactant fuel needed in each unit for escape tangent. The escape time, combining orbital speeds of Tara and Junior, are completed, and we have six hours and fifty-five minutes before blast-off!" He turned and rumpled Alfie's hair. "Alfie and I have completed the communications unit and have tested it. Junior is ready to get his big kick in the pants!"

Connel stood up. He was speechless. It was almost too much to believe.

"*Get below*," he roared, "and go to sleep! If I catch one of you awake in five minutes, I'll log you fifty demerits!"

The tired workers grinned back at their commander.

"I'll get everything set," said Connel, "and wake you up an hour before we have to get things ready. Now *hit the sack!*"

Their grins spreading even wider on their haggard faces, they turned away. Connel stepped to the desk on the control deck and wrote across the face of the logbook page.

"... October 2nd, 2353. Space Cadets Corbett, Manning, Astro, and Higgins and ex-enlisted spaceman Nicholas Shinny completed this day all preparation for operation Junior's Pitch. By authority vested in me as Senior Officer, Solar Guard, I hereby recommend official commendation of "*well done*" to the above-mentioned spacemen, and that all honors pursuant to that commendation be officially bestowed on them. Signed, Connel, Major, SO—SG ..."

He closed the book and wiped the corners of his eyes with the back of his hand.

CHAPTER 16

Well, fellows," said Tom, stifling a yawn, "it looks like we did it. But I could use some more sleep. That five hours was just enough to get started on!"

"Yeah," agreed Roger sourly, "but where does this Venusian lummox get off grabbing all the credit." He looked at Astro. "If I hadn't built the fuses for your little firecrackers—"

"*Firecrackers!*" yelped Astro. "Why, you skinny space fake! If I hadn't built those nuclear reactors, *you* wouldn't have anything to set off!"

Connel appeared in the small messroom of the *Polaris*, his hands full of papers and drawings. "When you've finished congratulating each other, I'd like to say a few things!" he snapped.

"Congratulate *him*?" exclaimed Roger. "Skipper, his head's so thick, the noise on the power deck can't even reach his eardrums!"

"Just one more word, Manning," growled Astro, "and I'll take a deep breath and blow you away!"

"*One more word out of either of you*," roared Connel, "and I'll throw you both in the brig with Mason and Loring!"

Suddenly he glared at the five spacemen. "Who's on prisoner watch today?" he asked.

The four cadets and Mr. Shinny looked at each other then at Roger.

"Uhhh—I am, sir," Roger confessed.

"I had a sneaking suspicion you would be!" said Connel. "Cadet Manning, one of the first things an officer of the Solar Guard learns is to care for the needs of his men and prisoners before himself. Did you know that, Cadet Manning?"

"Uhhh—yes, sir. I was just going to—" mumbled Roger.

"Then go below and see that Mason and Loring get their rations!"

"Yes, sir," said Roger. He got up and collected a tray of food.

"All of you report to the control deck in five minutes for briefing," said Connel and followed Roger out of the door.

"How do you like that?" said Astro. "We break our backs for the guy and we're no sooner finished then he starts the old routine again!"

"That has nothing to do with it, Astro," said Tom. "Put yourself in his position. We've only got one or two things to think about. He's responsible for it all."

"Just like he was when I sailed with him twenty-five years ago," said Shinny. He swallowed the remains of his tea and reached for a plug of tobacco. "He's all spaceman from the top of his head to the bottom of his space boots."

"I'm rather inclined to agree with you, Tom," said Alfie mildly. "Leadership carries with it the greatest of all burdens—responsibility for other peoples' lives. You, Corbett, as a control-deck cadet, would do well to mark Major Connel's pattern of behavior."

"Listen," growled Astro, "if Tom ever turned out to be a rocket buster like Connel—I'd—I'd—"

"Don't worry, Astro," Tom said, laughing. "I don't think there'll be another Major Connel in a million light years!"

Shinny laughed silently, his small frame shaking slightly. "Say it again, Tommy. Not in the whole universe will there ever be another like old 'Blast-off' Connel!"

On the deck below the messroom, Roger, balancing a tray carefully on one hand, opened the electronic lock of the brig and then stepped back quickly, leveling a paralo-ray gun.

"All right, Mason, Loring," he yelled, "come and get it!" The door slid open, and Loring stuck his head out. "Any funny business," Roger warned, "and I'll stiffen you so fast, you won't know what hit you!"

"It's about time you showed up!" growled Loring. "Whaddaya trying to do, starve us to death?"

"That's not a bad idea!" said Roger. Loring took the tray. Roger motioned him back inside the brig and slammed the door shut. He locked it and leaned against the grille.

"Better eat it while you can," he said. "They don't serve it so fancy on a prison asteroid."

"You'll never get us on a prison asteroid," whined Mason.

"Don't kid yourself," said Roger. "As soon as we get the reactor units set, we're going to send this hunk of copper back to Earth and then take you back. They'll bury you!"

"Who's going to do all that?" snapped Loring. "A bunch of punk kids and a loudmouthed Solar Guard officer?"

"Yeah," retorted Roger.

"*Cadet Manning!*" Connel's voice roared over the intercom. "You were ordered to report to the control deck in five minutes! You are already one minute late! Report to the control deck on the double and *I mean double!*"

Loring and Mason laughed. "Old 'Blast-off' Connel's really got your number, eh, kid?"

"Ah, rocket off, you pinheaded piece of space junk! It didn't take him long to dampen *your* tubes!"

Connel roared again. "*Blast your hide, Manning, report!*"

"Better raise ship, Manning," said Loring, "you might get another nasty demerit!"

Roger turned away and raced to the control deck. He entered breathlessly and stood beside his unit-mates while Connel eyed him coldly.

"Thank you, Cadet Manning," said Connel. "We appreciate your being here!"

"Yes, sir," mumbled Roger.

"All right," barked Connel, "you know your assignments. We'll take the jet boats as before and go out in pairs. Tom and myself, Astro and Roger, and Shinny and Alfie. We'll set up the reaction charges on Junior at the points marked on the chart screen here." He indicated the chart on the projection. "Copy them down on your own charts. Each team will take three of the reaction units. My team will set up at points one, two, and three. Astro and Roger at four, five, and six. Alfie and Shinny at seven, eight, and nine. After you've set up the charges, attach the triggers for the fuses and return to the ship. Watch your timing! If we fail, it'll be more than a year before Junior will be in the same orbital position again. How much time do we have left, Corbett?"

Tom glanced at the clock. "Exactly two hours, sir," he said.

"Not much," said Connel, "but enough. It shouldn't take more than an hour and a half to set up the units and get back to the ship to blast off. All clear? Any questions?"

There were no questions.

"All right," said the officer, "put on your space gear and move out!"

Handling the lead-encased charges carefully, the six spacemen loaded the jet boats and, one by one, blasted off from the *Polaris* to positions marked on the map.

Working rapidly, each of the teams of two moved from one position to another on the surface of the desolate satellite. Connel, referring constantly to his watch, counted the minutes as one by one the teams reported the installation of a reactor unit.

"This is Shinny. Just finished installing reaction charge one at point seven ..."

"This is Manning. Just finished installing reaction charge at point four ..."

One after the other, the teams reported. Connel, with Tom piloting the jet boat, finished setting up their units at points one, two, and three and headed back to the *Polaris*.

"How much time, sir?" asked Tom as he slowed the small craft for a landing.

"Less than a half hour, Corbett," said Connel nervously. "I'd better check on Shinny and Alfie." He called into the audiophone. "Major Connel to Shinny and Higgins, come in Shinny—Higgins!"

"Shinny here!" came the reply. "We're just finishing up the last unit. Should be back in five minutes."

"Make it snappy!" said Connel. "Less than a half hour left!"

"We'll make it," snorted Shinny.

"Coming in for a touchdown," said Tom. "Better strap in, sir!"

Connel nodded. He laced several straps across his lap and chest, gripping the sides of the seat. Tom sent the jet boat in a swooping dive, cut the acceleration, and brought the small ship smoothly inside the huge air lock in the side of the *Polaris*.

"I'd better get right up on the control deck and start warming up the circuits, sir," said Tom.

"Good idea, Tom," said Connel. "I'll try and pick up Manning and Astro."

Tom left the officer huddling over the communicator in the jet boat.

"Major Connel to Manning and Astro, come in!" called Connel. He waited for a moment and then repeated. "Manning—Astro, come in! By the rings of Saturn, come in!" There was the loud roar of an approaching jet boat. Shinny guided the ship into the *Polaris* with a quick violent blast of the braking rockets. The noise was deafening.

"Belay that noise, you blasted space-brained idiot!" roared Connel. "Cut that acceleration!"

Shinny grinned and cut the rockets. The jet-boat catapult deck was quiet, and Connel turned back to the communicator.

"Come in, Manning—Astro! This is Major Connel. Come in!"

On the opposite side of the airless satellite, Roger and Astro were busy digging a hole in the hard surface. Near by lay the last of the explosive units to be installed. Connel's voice thundered through their headset phones.

"Boy, is he blasting his jets!" commented Roger.

"Yeah," grunted Astro. "He should have to dig this blasted hole!"

"Well, this is where it's got to go. If the ground is hard, then it's our tough luck," said Roger. "If we stick it anywhere else, it might mess up the whole operation."

Astro nodded and continued to dig. He held a small spade and jabbed at the ground. "How much—time—have we got left?" he gasped.

"Twenty minutes," replied Roger. "You'd better hurry."

"Finished now," said Astro. "Get the reactor unit over here and set the fuse."

Roger picked up the heavy lead box and placed it gently inside the hole.

"Remember," Astro cautioned, "set the fuse for two hours."

"No, you're wrong," replied Roger. "I've set the fuses each time, subtracting the amount of time since we left the *Polaris*. I set this one for twenty minutes."

"You're wrong, Roger," said Astro. "It's maximum time is two hours."

"Listen, you Venusian clunk," exploded Roger, "*I* built this thing, so I know what I'm doing!"

"But, Roger—" protested Astro.

"Twenty minutes!" said Roger, and twisted the set-screw in the fuse. "O.K., it's all set. Let's get out of here!"

The two cadets raced back to the jet boat and blasted off immediately. Once in space, Astro turned to Roger.

"Better check in with Major Connel before he tears himself to pieces!"

"Yeah," agreed Roger. "I guess you're right." He flipped on the audio communicator. "Attention! Attention! Manning to Major Connel. Am making flight back to *Polaris*. All installations complete."

"Remember," Astro cautioned, "set the fuse for two hours."

"What took you so long, Manning?" barked Connel in reply. "And why didn't you answer me?"

"Couldn't, sir," said Roger. "We had a tough time digging a hole for the last unit."

"Come back to the *Polaris* immediately," said Connel. "We're blasting off in fifteen minutes."

"Very well, sir," said Roger.

Presently the jet boat circled the *Polaris* and made a landing run for the open port. Roger braked the small craft and brought it to rest alongside the others.

"That's it, spaceboy," he said to Astro. "All out for the *Polaris* express back home!"

"Just be sure you give me a good course, Manning," grunted Astro, heaving his huge frame out of the small cabin of the jet boat, "and I'll give you all the thrust you want!"

Astro secured the jet boats while Roger closed the air-lock hatch, shutting out the last view of the rugged little planetoid. Roger threw the landscape a mocking kiss.

"So long, Junior! See you back home!" The two cadets climbed the ladder leading to the control deck.

Seated in front of the control panel, Tom watched the sweeping hand of the solar clock. Connel paced nervously up and down behind him. Shinny and Alfie stood to one side also watching the great clock.

"How much time, Corbett?" asked Connel for the dozenth time.

"Junior gets his kick in the pants in ten minutes, sir," replied Tom.

"Fine," said Connel. "That gives me just enough time to notify Space Academy to get ready to receive Junior's signal. You know what to do?"

"I don't have to do anything, sir," answered Tom, nodding to the solar clock over his head. "In nine minutes and twenty seconds, the reactor units go off automatically at one-second intervals."

Roger and Astro entered the control deck and came to attention. Connel returned their salute and put them at ease.

"All right, our work here is done," said Connel. "No point in hanging around any longer. Tom, you can blast off immediately."

"Yes, sir," replied Tom.

Connel climbed the ladder to the radar bridge to contact Space Academy. Astro, Roger, Shinny, and Alfie went to their posts and began quick preparations for the blast-off. One by one, they checked in to Tom on the control deck.

"Power deck, ready to blast off!" reported Astro.

"Radar bridge, all set. Clear trajectory forward and up," said Roger.

"Energize the cooling pumps!" bawled Tom into the intercom.

The great pumps began to wheeze under the strain of Astro's sudden switch to full load without the usual slow build-up. Tom watched the pressure needle rise slowly in front of him and finally reached out and gripped the master switch.

"Stand by to raise ship!" he yelled.

"Blast off minus five—four—three—two—one—*zeroooooo!*"

He threw the switch. The great ship shivered, vibrated, and then suddenly shot away from the precious satellite. Tom quickly adjusted for free fall by switching on the synthetic-gravity gyro generators and then announced over the intercom,

"Major Connel! Cadet Corbett reporting. Ship space-borne at exactly thirty-one, sir!"

"Very well, Corbett," replied Connel. "Space Academy sends the crew a '*well done!*' Everything's set back home to take over the beam as soon as Junior starts on his way back. How much time until zero blast-off on the satellite?"

Tom glanced at the clock. "Less than two minutes, sir!"

"All right," said Connel over the intercom, "everybody to the control deck if you want to see Junior do his stuff!"

In a moment the six spacemen were gathered around the magnascope waiting for the final act of their great effort. Breathlessly, their eyes flicking back and forth from the solar clock to the magnascope, they waited for the red hand to sweep around.

"Here it comes," said Tom excitedly.

"One second—two seconds—three—four—*five!*"

On the surface of the planetoid, giant mushrooming clouds appeared climbing into the airless void. One by one the reactor units exploded. Connel counted them as they blew up.

"One, two, three, four, five, six, seven, eight—" he paused. Junior began moving away from them. "Nine!" shouted Connel. "What happened to nine?"

"Roger," shouted Astro, "you made a mistake on the timer!"

"But I couldn't. I—I—"

Connel spun around, his eyes blazing, breathing hard. "What time did you set the last one for, Roger?" he demanded.

"Why, twenty minutes to blast-off time, sir," answered the blond-headed cadet.

"Then it won't go off for another forty minutes," said Connel.

"But, sir—" began Roger, and then fell silent. The room was quiet. Everyone looked at Roger and then at Connel. "Honestly, sir, I didn't mean to make a mistake. I—" pleaded Roger.

Connel turned around. His face suddenly looked very tired. "That's all right, Roger," he said quietly. "We've all been working pretty hard. One little mistake is bound to show up in an operation like this." He paused. "It's my fault. I should have checked those fuses myself."

"Does it make so much difference, sir?" asked Astro.

"A lot of difference, Astro," said Connel. He sat down heavily.

"But how, sir?" asked Tom.

"It's very simple, Tom," answered Connel. His voice was strangely quiet. "Junior spins on its axis in two hours, just as Earth spins in twenty-four hours. I thought we had the explosions timed so at the proper moment we'd push Junior out of his orbit around Tara, and the greater orbit around Alpha Centauri, by utilizing both speeds, plus the initial thrust. But by being one blast short, forty minutes late, the explosion will take place when Junior is forty minutes out of position"—he paused and calculated rapidly in his mind—"that's about forty-eight thousand miles out of position. When it goes off, instead of sending Junior out into space, it'll blast it right into its own sun!"

"Isn't there something we can do, sir?" asked Tom.

"Nothing, Corbett," answered Connel wearily. "Instead of supplying the Solar Alliance with copper, in another week Junior will be hardly more than a molten piece of space junk." He looked at the teleceiver screen. All ready, Junior was falling away. "Stand by for full acceleration, hyperdrive," said the big officer in a hoarse whisper. "We're heading home!"

CHAPTER 17

The subdued whine of the hyperdrive filled the power deck and made Roger wince as he stepped through the hatch and waved at Astro. He climbed down the ladder and stopped beside the big Venusian who stood stripped to the waist, watching the pressure gauges on the power-deck control board.

"Hiya, Roger," said Astro with a big grin.

"Hello, Astro," replied Roger and sat down on a stool near by.

"Excuse me a minute, hot-shot," said Astro. "Gotta check the baffling around reaction tube three." The big cadet hurriedly donned a lead-lined protective suit and entered the reaction chamber. After a moment he reappeared and took off the suit. He poured a glass of water, handed it to Roger, and poured another for himself.

"Gets pretty hot down here," he said. "I don't like to use the air conditioner when I'm on hyperdrive. Sucks my power output and reduces pressure on the oxygen pumps."

Roger nodded absently at the needlessly detailed explanation. Astro looked at him sharply. "Say, what's eating you?"

"Honestly, Astro," said Roger, "I've never felt more miserable in my life."

"Don't let it get you down, Roger," said Astro. "The major said it was a mistake anyone could make."

"Yeah," flared Roger, "but have you seen the way he just—*talks*?"

"Talks?" asked Astro blankly.

"Yeah, talks," said Roger. "No yelling, or blasting off, or handing out demerits like they were candy. Nothing! Why he hasn't even chewed Alfie out since we left Junior. He just sits in his quarters."

Astro understood now and nodded his head in agreement. "Yeah, you're right.

I'd rather have him fusing his tubes than the way he is now."

"Tom must feel pretty rotten, too," said Roger. "I haven't seen much of him either."

"Or Alfie," put in Astro. "Neither of them have done anything but work. I don't think either of them has slept since we left Tara."

"It's all my fault!" said Roger. "I'm nothing but a loudmouthed bag of space gas—with an asteroid for a head!" He got up and lurched toward the ladder.

"Hey, where you going?" yelled Astro.

"Almost forgot," yelled Roger from the top of the ladder. "I've got to feed our prisoners a meal. And the way I feel, I'd like to shove it down their throats!"

Roger went directly to the galley off the control deck and prepared a hasty meal for Loring and Mason. He piled it on a tray and went below to the brig.

"All right, Loring," he growled, "come and get it!"

"Well, well, well," sneered Loring. "Where's the big Manning spirit? You boys are kinda down since you blew that little operation, huh?"

"Listen, you space crawler," said Manning coldly, "one more word out of you and I'll bring you out in the passageway and pound that head of yours into space junk!"

"I wish you'd try that, you little squirt!" snarled Loring. "I'd break you in two!"

"O.K., pal," said Roger, "I'm going to give you that chance!" He opened the door to the cell and Loring stepped out. Holding the paralo-ray gun on him, Roger relocked the door. Left inside, Mason stuck his face close to the grille.

"Give it to him, Loring," he hissed. "Take him apart!"

Roger threw the paralo-ray gun in the corner of the passageway and faced the heavier spaceman. He held his arms loosely at his side, and he balanced on the balls of his feet. A slight smile played at the corners of his mouth.

"Start breaking, Loring," he said quietly.

"Why, you—" snarled Loring and rushed in. He swung wildly for Roger's head, but the cadet slipped inside the punch and drove a hard right to Loring's mid-section. The prisoner doubled over, staggered back, and slowly straightened up. Roger's lips were drawn tightly in a grimace of cold anger. His eyes were shining hard and bright. He stepped in quickly and chopped two straight lefts to Loring's jaw, then doubled the spaceman up again with a hard right to the heart. Loring gasped and tried to clinch. But Roger threw a straight jolting right to his jaw. The prisoner slumped to the floor, out cold. The fight was finished.

Roger went over, picked up the paralo-ray gun, and opened the cell door again.

"All right, Mason," he said coldly, "drag him inside. And if you want to try me for size, just say so."

Mason didn't answer. He merely hurried out, and grabbing Loring by the feet, dragged him inside. Roger slammed the door and locked it.

Rubbing his knuckles and feeling better than he had felt for days, he started back to the radar bridge. As he neared Major Connel's quarters, he heard Connel's voice. He stopped and listened outside the door.

"It's a beautiful job of calculation, Tom," Connel was saying. "I don't see how you and Higgins could have done it in so short a time. And without an electronic computer to aid you. Beautiful job—really excellent—but I'm afraid it's too risky."

"I've already talked to Astro and Mr. Shinny, sir," said Tom, "and they've volunteered. I haven't spoken to Roger yet, but I'm sure he'd be willing to try."

Roger stepped through the door.

"Whatever it is," said Roger, "I'm ready."

"Eavesdropping on your commanding officer," said Connel, eying the blond-headed cadet speculatively, "is a very serious offense."

"I just happened to hear my name mentioned, sir," replied Roger with a smile.

Connel turned back to Tom. "Go over that again, Tom."

"Well, sir," said Tom, "Junior's falling into the sun at a speed of twenty-two miles a second right now. But we could still land a jet boat on Junior, set up more nuclear explosions to blast him out of the sun's grip, and send him on his way to our solar system. We wouldn't get as much speed as before, but we'd still save the copper."

By this time, Astro and Shinny had joined the group and were standing outside the door in the passageway, listening silently.

Connel tugged at his chin. "Let's see," he said, "if we could get back to Tara in three days ..." He looked up at Astro. "Do you think you could get us back in three days, Astro?"

"Major Connel, for another crack at Junior," roared the big Venusian, "I'd get you back in a day and a half!"

"All right," said Connel. "That's one problem. But there are others."

"What, sir?" asked Tom.

"We have to prepare reactant fuses and we have to build new reactor units. If we could do that—"

"If Astro can get us back," said Shinny, "and Roger and this smart young feller here, Alfie, can make up some fuses, I'll build them there units. After all, Astro showed me how once. I guess I can follow his orders!"

"Good!" said Connel. "Now there is the element of time. How much time would we need on Junior?" He looked at Tom.

"Let me answer this way, sir," said Tom. "We'd only have two hours to plant the reaction charges and trigger them, but that should be enough."

"Why so close, Tom?" asked Roger.

"It has to be," answered Tom. "We know what the pull of the sun is, and the power of the jet boat. When the sun's pull becomes greater than the escape speed of the jet boat, the boat would never clear. It would keep falling into the sun. I've based this figure on reaching Junior at the last possible moment."

"It'd take at least five men to set up the five explosions we need," mused Connel. "That means one of us will have to stay on the *Polaris*."

There was an immediate and loud chorus of "Not me!" from everyone.

"All right," said Connel, "we'll draw numbers. One, two, three, four, five, and six. The man who draws number six will stay with the *Polaris*. All right?"

"Yes, sir," said Tom, glancing around. "We agree to that."

Connel went to his desk and wrote quickly on six slips of paper. He folded each one, dumped them in his cap, and offered it to Astro.

"All right, Astro," said Connel, "draw!"

Astro licked his lips and stuck in his big paw. The Venusian fingered several, then pulled out a slip of paper. He opened it and read aloud. "Number two! I go!" He turned and grinned at the others.

Connel offered his cap to Alfie. Alfie dipped in two fingers and pulled out a slip. "Number four! I go!" he squealed.

Roger and Shinny drew numbers one and three. Tom looked at the major. "Go ahead, Corbett," said Connel.

"After you, sir," said Tom.

"I said draw one!" roared Connel.

"Yes, sir," said Tom. He reached in and quickly pulled out one of the two remaining slips.

"Number six," he said quietly. "I stay."

Connel, not bothering to open the last one, slapped the hat on his head and turned away.

"But, sir," said Tom, "I—ah—"

Connel cut him off with a wave of his hands. "No ***buts***!" He turned to the others. "Manning, Higgins! Get me a course back to Junior and make it clean and straight. Astro, Shinny, stand by on the power deck for course change. Tom, get on the control deck. We're going back to snatch a hot copper filling right out of a sun's teeth!"

Once again the energy of the six spacemen was burned in twenty-four hour stretches of improvisation and detailed calculations. Roger and Alfie redesigned the fuse to ensure perfect co-ordination of the explosions. Astro and Shinny surpassed their previous efforts by putting enough power in the five small reaction units to more than do the job required. Tom, standing long watches on the control deck, devoted his spare time to the torturous equations that would mean failure or success to the whole project. And Major Connel, alert and alive once more, drove his crew toward greater goals than it had achieved before.

Nearly three days later, the ***Polaris*** appeared over the twin oceans of Tara and glided into an orbit just beyond the pull of the planet's gravity. Aboard the spaceship, last-minute preparations were made by the red-eyed spacemen.

In constant contact with Space Academy, using the resources of the Academy's scientific staff to check the more difficult calculations, the six men on the ***Polaris*** worked on.

Connel appeared on the radar bridge and flipped on the long-range scanner.

"Have to find out where Junior is," he said to Roger and Alfie.

"That doesn't work, sir," said Roger.

"What do you mean it doesn't work?" exploded Connel.

"Junior's falling into the sun, sir. The radiations are blocking it out from our present position."

"Couldn't we move to another position?" asked the officer.

"Yes, sir," said Roger, "we could. But to do that would take extra time, and we haven't got it."

"Then how are you going to find Junior?" asked Connel.

"Alfie's busy with a special scanner, sir, one that's especially sensitive to copper. Since the sun is composed mostly of gas, with this filter only Junior will show up on the screen."

"By the rings of Saturn," exclaimed Connel, "you mean to tell me that Alfie

Higgins is building a new radar scanner, just like that?"

"Why, yes, sir," answered Roger innocently. "Is there something wrong with that?"

"No—no—" said Connel, backing off the bridge. "Just—just go right on. You're doing fine! Yessirree, fine!" He literally ran from the bridge.

"Most humorous of you, Manning," said Alfie, smiling.

"I'll tell you something funnier than that," said Roger. "I feel the same way he does. Is there anything you *can't* do, Alfie?"

Alfie thought a moment. "Yes, there is," he said at last.

"What?" demanded Roger.

"I can't—shall I say?—make as much progress as you do with—er—space dolls."

Roger's jaw dropped. "Space dolls! You mean—girls?"

Alfie nodded his head.

"Listen," said Roger, "when we get Junior on his way home, and we get back to the Academy, I promise you I'll show you how to really blast your jets with the space lovelies in Atom City!"

Alfie put out his hand seriously. "And if you do that for me, Roger, I'll show you how to use the new electronic brain they recently acquired at the Academy. Only one other person can operate it. But you definitely have the potential."

Roger stared at him stupidly. "Huh? Yeah. Oh, sure!"

Gradually the mass of data was brought together and co-ordinated, and finally, as Tom stood beside him, Major Connel checked over his calculations.

"I can't see a thing wrong with it, Tom," Connel said at last. "I guess that's it. Figuring we land on Junior at exactly seventeen hundred hours, we'd reach the point of no return exactly two hours later."

"Shall I alert stations to blast off for Junior?" asked Tom.

"Yes," said Connel, "bring the *Polaris* to dead ship in space about three hundred miles above Junior. That's when we'll blast off in jet boats."

"Yes, sir," said Tom. His eyes bright, he turned to the intercom. "All right, you space babies," he announced, "this is it. Stand by to blast Junior. Here we come!"

CHAPTER 18

Dawn broke over the tangled jungles of Tara, followed by the bright sun of Alpha Centauri rising out of the eastern sea and slowly climbing higher and higher. In the dense unexplored wilderness, living things, terrible things, opened their eyes and resumed their never-ending quest for food. Once again Alpha Centauri had summoned one hemisphere of its satellite planet to life.

Meanwhile, high in the heavens above Tara, six Earthmen blasted into the flaming brilliance of the sun star. Using delicate instruments instead of claws, and their intelligence instead of blind hunger, they prepared to do battle with the sun star and force it to release the precious copper satellite from its deadly, consuming grasp.

The crew of the *Polaris* assembled on the control deck of the great spaceship, and facing their commanding officer, waited patiently for the word that would send them hurtling out to their target.

"The jet boats are all ready, sir," reported Tom. "We're dead ship in orbit around Junior at an altitude of about three hundred miles."

"Does that mean we're falling into the sun too?" gasped Shinny.

"It sure does, Mr. Shinny," said Alfie, "at more than twenty miles per second."

"The jet boats have enough power to get back from Junior to the *Polaris*, Mr. Shinny," reassured Tom. "And then the *Polaris* can blast off from here. The jet boats wouldn't go much higher off Junior this close to the sun."

"But if we go beyond the two-hour limit, the *Polaris* can't blast off either," commented Roger dryly.

"All right. Is everything set?" asked Connel. "Astro, is the reactant loaded?"

"No, sir," said Astro, "but it's all ready to go in."

"Good!" said Connel. "Now we all know how important—and how dangerous—this operation is. I don't have to tell you again. You stay here on the control deck, Tom, and keep in touch with us on Junior at all times. You know what to do?"

"Yes, sir," replied Tom. "I'm to stand by and give you a minute-by-minute warning check until final blast-off time."

"Right," said Connel. "And remember, we're counting on you to tell us when to blast off. We'll be too busy down there to pay any attention."

"I understand, sir," replied Tom. His face was passive. He was well aware of the responsibility.

"Very well," said Connel finally, "the rest of you board your jet boats! This is going to be the hottest ride we'll ever take, and I don't want it to get any hotter!"

Silently, their faces grim masks, the five spacemen filed out of the control room, leaving Tom alone. Presently he heard the cough of the rockets in the jet boats as one by one the small space craft blasted out of the *Polaris*. Suddenly Tom began to shake as he realized the importance of his task—the responsibility of counting time for five men, time that could cost them their lives. If he made a single mistake, miscounted by a minute, the expedition to Junior would end not only in failure, but in tragedy.

As quickly as the thought came, Tom pushed it aside and turned to the control board. No time now for fear. Now, more than any other time in his life, he had to keep himself alert and ready for every emergency. As a child he had often dreamed of the day when, as a spaceman, he would be faced with an emergency only he could handle. And in the dreams he had come through with flying colors. But now that it was a reality, Tom felt nothing but cold sweat breaking out on his forehead.

He turned his whole attention to the great solar clock overhead. Time had already begun slipping away. Ten minutes of the two hours had swept past. They must be on Junior by now, he thought, and flipped on the teleceiver. He focused on the satellite's surface. There in front of him were the three jet boats. Major Connel, Roger, Astro, Alfie, and Mr. Shinny were so close that Tom felt as though he could touch them. They were unloading the first reactor unit, with Astro and Shinny digging the hole. Tom glanced at the clock, turned to the microphone, and announced clearly:

"Attention! Attention! Corbett to Connel. One hour and forty-eight minutes until blast-off time—one hour and forty-eight minutes to blast-off."

He flipped the switch and watched the screen with rising excitement. The crew on the satellite had completed the installation of the first reactor unit. He saw them blasting off in their jet boats for the second spot. He adjusted the teleceiver and tried to follow them, but they disappeared. He glanced at the clock.

"Attention! Attention! Corbett to Connel. One hour and forty-seven minutes to blast-off—one hour and forty-seven minutes to blast-off."

On the satellite, in the deep shadow of a protecting cliff, each of the five Earthmen paused involuntarily when they heard Tom's warning.

"Forget about the time!" snapped Connel. "By the blessed rings of Saturn, we'll finish this job if it's the last thing we do!"

Connel went to each of the working figures and adjusted the valve, regulating the air-cooling humidity control on their space suits. "Getting pretty hot, eh, boys?" he joked, as he stopped one and then the other to make the delicate adjustment counteracting the heat that was increasing each second they remained on the satellite.

"How hot do you think it is, sir?" asked Roger.

"Never mind the heat," said Connel. "These suits were designed to withstand the temperature of the light side of Mercury! It gets boiling there, so I guess we can stand it here for a while."

One by one, Alfie, Shinny, Roger, and Astro completed their assigned roles, digging the holes, placing the reactors inside, setting the fuse, covering it up, then quickly gathering the equipment, piling back into the three jet boats, and heading for the next point. Landing, they would tumble out of the small space craft almost before the rocket had stopped firing and begin their frantic digging in the hard surface.

Over and over, they heard Tom's crisp clear count of time. Five minutes passed, then ten, and before they knew it, a full half-hour of the precious time had vanished. They completed the installation of the second unit and climbed back into the jet boats. The first two units had been buried at points protected from the sun by cliffs, and they had been sheltered from the burning rays.

Landing, they would tumble out of the jet boat and begin their frantic digging

But, approaching the position for the third reactor unit, Connel searched in vain for some shade. He wasted five precious minutes, scouting an area of several miles, but he could find nothing to protect them on the flat plain.

"Better put in the ultraviolet glass shields in our helmets, boys," he called into the jet-boat communicator. "It's going to be mighty hot, and dangerous."

"Aye, aye, sir," came the replies from the other two jet boats soaring close by.

Roger began refitting their space helmets with the dark glass that would shield them from the strong rays of the enlarging sun.

"Ever been outside in the direct path of the sun with no protection, Roger?" asked Astro.

"No," replied Roger. "Have you?"

"Once," said Astro softly. "On the second moon of Mars, Phobos. I was bucking rockets on the old chemical burners. I was on a freighter called the *Happy Spaceman*. A tube blew on us. Luckily we were close enough to Phobos to make a touchdown, or the leak would have reached the main fuel tanks and blown us clean out to another galaxy."

"What happened?" asked Roger.

"I had to go outside," said Astro. "I was junior rocketman in the crew, so naturally I had to do all the dirty work."

Tom's warning call from the *Polaris* control deck, tuned to the open communicators of all the jet boats, broke through the loud-speaker.

"Attention! Attention! Corbett to Connel. One hour and twenty minutes to blast-off time. One hour and twenty minutes to blast-off time."

The two cadets looked at each other as they heard Tom's voice, but neither spoke. Finally Roger asked, "What happened on Phobos?"

"No one bothered to tell me," continued Astro, "that I had to protect myself from the ultraviolet rays of the sun, since Phobos didn't have an atmosphere. It was one of my first hops into space and I didn't know too much. I went outside and began working on the tube. I did the job all right, but for three weeks after, my face was swollen and I couldn't open my eyes. I almost went blind."

Roger grunted and continued to line the clear plastic fish-bowl helmets with the darker protective shields.

Connel's voice rang through the cabin over the communicator: "I guess we'd better go down and get it over with. I don't see anything that will give us any protection down there. Be sure your humidity control is turned up all the way. As soon as you step outside the jet boat, you're going to be hit by a temperature of four hundred degrees!"

"Aye, aye, sir," came Shinny's reply over the intercom. Roger flipped the communicator on and acknowledged the order.

Astro and Shinny followed Connel's jet boat in a long sweeping dive to the surface of the satellite. Stepping out of the air-cooled jet boat onto the torrid unprotected surface of the flat plain was like stepping into a furnace. Even with space suits as protection, the five Earthmen were forced to work in relays in the digging of the hole for the reactor unit.

"Attention! Attention! Corbett to Connel. One hour exactly to blast-off time! One hour—sixty minutes—to blast-off time."

Tom flicked the teleceiver microphone off, and on the teleceiver screen, watched his spacemates work under the broiling sun. They were ahead of time. One hour to complete two more units. Tom allowed himself a sigh of hope and relief. They could still snatch the copper satellite from the powerful pull of the sun.

Suddenly Tom heard a sound behind him and whirled around. His eyes bulged in horror.

"Loring!" he gasped.

"Take your hand off that microphone, Corbett," snarled Loring, "or I'll freeze you!"

"How—how did you get out?" Tom stammered.

"Your buddy, Manning," sneered Loring with a short laugh, "decided he wanted to paste my ears back. So I let him. He was so anxious to make me lose a few teeth that he didn't notice the spoon I kept!"

"Spoon?" asked Tom incredulously.

"Yeah," said Mason, stepping through the door, a paralo-ray gun leveled at Tom. "A few teeth for a spoon. A good trade. We waited for your pals to leave the ship, and then I short-circuited the electronic lock on the brig."

Tom stared at the two men unbelievingly.

"All right, Corbett, get over there to that control board," growled Loring, waving the paralo-ray gun at Tom. "We're going back to Tara."

"Tara?" exclaimed Tom. "But Major Connel and the others—they're—they're down on the satellite. If I don't pick them up, they'll fall into the sun!"

"Well, ain't that too bad," sneered Loring. "Listen to that, Mason. If we don't hang around and pick them up, they'll fall into the sun!"

Mason laughed harshly and advanced toward Tom. "I only got one regret, Corbett. That I can't stay around to see Connel and the Manning punk fry! Now get this wagon outta here, and get it out quick!"

CHAPTER 19

M ajor!" shouted Astro. "Look! The **Polaris**! The **Polaris** is blasting off!"

The five Earthmen stared up at the silvery spaceship that was rapidly disappearing into the clear blue void of space. Without hesitation, Connel raced for the nearest jet boat and roared into the communicator.

"Corbett! Corbett! Come in, Tom!"

He waited, the silence of the loud-speaker more menacing than anything the spaceman had ever encountered before. Again and again, the Solar Guard officer tried to raise the cadet on the **Polaris**. Finally he turned back to the four crewmen who hovered around the jet boat, hoping against hope.

"Whatever it is," he said, "I'm sure Tom is doing the right thing. We came down here to do a job and we're going to do it! Get moving! We still have to set up the rest of these reactor units."

Without a word, the five men returned to their small ships and followed their commanding officer.

The sun grew larger and the heat more intense with each minute, since each minute brought them almost thirteen hundred miles closer to the sun's blazing surface. With the humidity-control and air-cooling mechanisms in the space suits working at top capacity but affording little relief, Alfie, Roger, Shinny, and Astro buried the fourth reactor unit and headed for the fifth and last emplacement. Occasionally one of them would turn and cast a swift glance at the clear blue space overhead, secretly hoping to find the rocket cruiser had returned. Or, they would strain their ears for Tom's voice counting off the minutes so carefully for them. But they saw nothing and they heard nothing. They concentrated on their jobs, work-ing like demons to complete the installations as planned. They could not stop now and wonder what had happened to the *Polaris*, or even hope for its speedy return. They had a job to do, and they went about it silently, efficiently, and surely.

Astro stood up, the small spade in his hand hanging loosely at his side. He watched Roger and Alfie bring the last of the reactor units from Major Connel's jet boat. They gently lowered it into the hole and stepped back while Shinny, under the watchful eyes of Major Connel, set the fuse. Shinny stepped back, and Astro began covering up the lead box.

"That's it," said Connel. "We're finished!"

What Connel meant was that they were finished with the placement of the reactor units, but he knew immediately that his words had been taken to mean something each felt but had not dared to put into words.

Connel started to correct this misunderstanding but caught himself in time. It would not do, he thought, for him to make excuses for what they knew to be the truth.

"All right, everyone in my jet boat," he snapped. "Astro, you and Roger take all the fuel out of the other boats and pour it into mine. It'll be a tight squeeze, but we can all fit into one craft. No use expending fuel wastefully."

Astro and Roger bent to the task of draining the fuel from their jet boats and loading it into Connel's.

Alfie came over to join them, while Shinny and Connel scanned the sky overhead for some sign of the *Polaris*.

"This is really a desperate situation to be in, isn't it, Roger?" asked Alfie.

"Offhand, I'd say yes," drawled Roger, "but since we've got two big huskies like Astro and Major Connel along, I don't think we'll have much trouble."

"Why not?" asked Alfie.

"We'll just let them get out and help push!"

"And if that doesn't work," snorted Astro, "we'll stick Manning outside and let him talk about himself. That oughta give us enough gas to get us away from this hunk of copper."

"I believe," said Alfie emphatically, "that you're joshing me, Manning."

"Now, whatever gave you that idea?" asked Roger in a hurt tone.

"This *is* a serious situation, isn't it?" asked Alfie, looking at Astro.

"It sure is, Alfie," said Astro soberly, "and I'm the first one to say I'm a little scared!"

Alfie smiled. "I'm very glad you said that, Astro," he said, "because I feel exactly the same way!" He turned and walked back to Major Connel.

"What was the idea of telling him that?" hissed Roger at Astro. "What are you trying to do? Get the little guy space happy, or something?"

"Look at him!" said Astro. "I'm twice his size. He figures if a big guy like me is scared, then he's got a right to be scared too!"

Roger grunted in appreciation of the way Astro had treated Alfie's fears and turned back to the loading of the fuel.

Major Connel walked over and watched them transfer the last of the fuel into the tanks.

"How much have you got there, Astro?" he asked.

"I'd say enough to sustain flight for about three hours, sir. Considering we'll have such a big load."

"Ummmmh," mused Connel. "You know we're up against big odds, don't you?"

Roger and Astro nodded.

"If Tom doesn't come back soon, we'll be so far into the pull of the sun, even a ship the size of the *Polaris* wouldn't be able to break out."

"How much time have we got, sir?" asked Roger.

"Not too much, Manning," said Connel. "Of course we can blast off in the jet boat and get up a few hundred miles, in case Tom does come back. Then he won't have to bring the *Polaris* down here. But if time runs out on us up there, we'll have to come back and take our chance on Junior being blasted out of the sun's grip."

There was a pause while Astro and Roger considered this.

"That would mean," asked Roger, "that we'd be here when the reactor units go off, wouldn't it, sir?"

"That's right, Manning," said Connel, admitting to the danger. "Even if Junior were blasted out of the pull of the sun, we couldn't survive the explosions."

"Couldn't we blast off in the jet boat and then land after the explosions, sir?" asked Astro.

"Yes," admitted Connel, "we could do that. But the radioactivity would be so powerful we couldn't last more than a few days. We have no antiradiation gear. Not even food or water." He paused and scanned the sky. "No," he said in a surprisingly casual voice, "the only way we can get out of this is for Tom to come back and get us."

Shinny and Alfie came over and joined the group around the jet boat. No one said anything. There wasn't anything to say. Each of them felt the heat burning through his space suit. Each felt the same fear tugging at his throat. There was nothing to say. The *Polaris* was not to be seen; the sky was empty of everything except Alpha Centauri, the great burning mass of gases that once they had all seen only as a quiet twinkling star in the heavens, never dreaming that someday it would be pulling them relentlessly into its molten self.

Tom Corbett had a plan.

He sat at the control board of the great rocket cruiser, apparently watching the needles and gauges on the panel, but his mind was racing desperately. The two-hour deadline had just passed. The great solar clock had swung its red hand past the last second. Only a miracle could save the five men on Junior now. But Tom was not counting on miracles. He was counting on his plan.

"Keep this space wagon driving, Corbett!" ordered Loring from behind him. "Keep them rockets wide open!"

"Listen, Loring," pleaded Tom. "How about giving those fellows a break? If I don't pick them up, they'll all be killed."

"Ain't that too bad," snarled Mason.

"Look," said Tom desperately, "I'll promise you nothing will happen to you. We'll let you go free. We'll—"

Loring cut him off. "Shut your trap and concentrate on them controls! You and Major Connel and them other punks are the only guys between me staying free or going back to a prison asteroid. So you don't think I'm going to let them stay alive, do you?" He grinned crookedly.

"You dirty space crawler!" growled Tom and suddenly leaped up from the control seat.

Loring raised the paralo-ray gun threateningly. "One more move outta you and I'll freeze you so solid you'll think you're a chunk of ice!" he yelled.

Mason stepped to the other side of the control deck. They had Tom blocked on either side.

"Now get back to them controls, Corbett," snarled Loring, "or I'll give it to you right now."

"O.K., Loring, you win," said Tom. He sat down and faced the control panel. He tried hard not to smile. They had fallen for it. Now they were separated. Mason remained on the opposite side of the room. Tom took a deep breath, crossed his fingers, and put the next step of his plan into action. He reached out and pulled the master acceleration switch all the way back. The *Polaris* jumped ahead as if shot out of a cannon.

"Hey," growled Mason, "what're you doing?"

"You want more speed, don't you?" demanded Tom.

"O.K.," said Mason, "but don't try any funny stuff!"

"I don't see how I can. You've got me nailed with that paralo-ray," Tom replied.

He got up leisurely, so as not to excite the nervous trigger finger of Loring, and turned slowly.

"What is it this time?" demanded Loring.

"I just gave you an extra burst of speed. All the *Polaris* will take. Now I've got to adjust the mixture of the fuel, otherwise she'll kick out on you and we'll have to clean out the tubes."

"Yeah," sneered Loring. "Well, I happen to know you do that right on the control board." He motioned with the paralo-ray gun. "Get back down!"

"On regular space drive, you do," agreed Tom. "But we're on hyperdrive now. It has to be done there"—he pointed to a cluster of valves and wheels at one side of the control deck—"one of those valve wheels."

"Stay where you are," said Mason. "I'll do it!" He moved to the corner. "Which one is it?" he asked.

Tom gulped and struggled hard to keep the terrible nervousness out of his voice. He had to sound as casual as possible. "The red one. Turn it to the right, hard!" he said.

Loring sat down and Mason bent over the valve wheel. He gave the wheel a vicious twist. Suddenly there was the sound of a motor slowing down somewhere inside the great ship. Tom gripped the edge of the control board and waited. Slowly at first, but surely, Tom felt himself beginning to float off his chair.

"Hey!" yelled Mason. "I'm—I'm floating!"

"It's the gravity generators," yelled Loring. "Corbett's pulled a fast one. We're in free fall!"

Tom lifted his feet and pushed as hard as he could against the control panel. He shot out of the chair and across the control room just as Loring fired his ray gun. There was a loud hiss as the gun was fired, and then the thud of a body against the wall, as Loring was suddenly shoved by the recoil of the charge.

Tom huddled in the upper corner of the control deck like a spider, his legs drawn up underneath him waiting for Mason to fire. But the smaller spaceman was tumbling head over heels in the center of the room. The more he exerted himself, the more helpless he became. His arms and legs splayed out in an effort to level himself, as he kept trying to fire the ray gun.

Tom saw his chance and lunged through the air again, straight at the floating spaceman. He passed him in mid-air. Mason made an attempt to grab him, but Tom wrenched his body to one side and pulled the ray gun out of the other's hand.

He flipped over and turned his attention to Loring who was more dangerous, since he was now backed up against a bulkhead waiting for Tom to present a steady target. Loring started to fire, but Tom saw him in time and shot away from the wall toward the hatch. He twisted his body completely around, and with his shoulder hunched over, fired at Loring with his ray gun. The charge hit the target and Loring became rigid, his body slowly floating above the deck. His back to the wall, braced for the recoil, Tom brought his arm around slowly and aimed at Mason. He fired, and the spaceman stiffened.

Tom smiled. Neither of the spacemen would give him any more trouble now. He pushed slightly to the left and shot over to the valve that Mason had unwittingly turned off. Tom turned it on and clung to an overhead pipe until he felt the reassuring grip of the synthetic gravity pull him to the deck. Loring and Mason, in the same positions they had been in when Tom fired, settled slowly to the deck. Tom walked over and looked at both of them. He knew they could hear him.

"For smart spacemen like you two," said Tom, "you sure forgot your basic physics. Newton's laws of motion, remember? Everything in motion tends to keep going at the same speed, unless influenced by an outside force. Firing the ray gun was the outside force that will land you right on a prison asteroid! And you'd better start praying that I can pull those fellows off that satellite, because if I don't, you'll wind up frying in the sun with us!"

He started to drag them to a locker and release them from the effects of the ray blast, but, remembering their cold-blooded condemnation of Connel and the others to death on the satellite, he decided to let them remain where they were.

He turned to the control board and flipped on the microphone. He was too far away to pick up an image on the teleceiver, but the others could hear him on the audio, if, thought Tom, they were still alive.

"Attention! Attention! *Polaris* to Major Connel! Major Connel, can you hear me? Come in, Major Connel—Astro—Roger—somebody—come in!"

He turned away from the mike and fired the starboard jets full blast, making a sweeping curve in space and heading the *Polaris* back to Junior.

CHAPTER 20

There's only one answer, boys," said Connel. "Loring and Mason have escaped and taken over the ship. I can't think of any other reason Tom would abandon us like this."

The jet boat was crowded. Alfie, the smallest, was sitting on Astro's lap. For more than an hour they had circled above the copper satellite, searching the surrounding skies in vain for some sign of the *Polaris*.

"Major," said Roger, who was hunched over the steering wheel of the small space craft, "we're almost out of fuel. We'd better drop down on the night side of Junior, the side away from the sun. At least there we'd be out of the direct heat."

"Very well, Roger," said Connel. "In fact, we could keep shifting into the night side every hour." Then he added quietly, thoughtfully, "But we're out of fuel, you said?"

"Yes, sir," said Roger. "There's just enough to get down." Roger sent the craft in a shallow dive. Suddenly the rockets cut out. The last of the fuel was gone. Roger glided the jet boat to a smooth stop on the night side of the planetoid.

"How much longer before the reactor units go up?" asked Shinny.

Connel turned, thinking he had heard something on the communicators, then answered Shinny's question. "Only four hours," he said.

The crew of spacemen climbed out of the jet boat into the still blackness of the night side of the planet. There wasn't anything left to do.

They sat around on the hard surface of the planet, staring at the strange stars overhead.

"You know," said Astro, "I might be able to set up something to convert some of the U235 in the reactors to fuel the jet boat."

"Impossible, Astro," said Alfie. "You'd need a reduction gear. And not only that, but you haven't any tools to handle the mass. If you opened one of those boxes, you'd be fried immediately by the radiation!"

"Alfie's right," said Connel. "There's nothing to do but wait."

Major Connel turned his face up as far as he could in the huge fish-bowl helmet to stare at the sky. His eyes wandered from star cluster to star cluster, from glowing Regulus, to bright and powerful Sirius. He stifled a sigh. How much he had wanted to see more—and more—and more of the great wide, high, and deep! He remembered his early days as a youth on his first trip to Luna City; his first sensation at touching an alien world; his skipper, old, wise, and patient, who had given him his creed as a spaceman: "Travel wide, deep, and high," the skipper had said to the young Connel, "but never so far, so wide, or so deep as to forget that you're an Earthman, or how to act like an Earthman!" Even now, years later, the gruff voice rang in his ears. It wasn't long after that that he had met Shinny. Connel smiled behind the protection of his helmet, as he looked at the wizened spaceman, who was now old and toothless, but who still had the same merry twinkle in his eye that Connel had noticed the first time he saw him. Connel had signed on as first officer on a deep spacer bound for Titan. Shinny had come aboard and reported to Connel as rocketman. Shinny had promptly started roaring through the passageways of the huge freighter in his nightshirt singing snatches of old songs at the top of his voice. It had taken Connel four hours to find where Shinny had hidden the bottle of rocket juice! Connel laughed. He looked over at the old man fondly.

"Say, Nick," said Connel, addressing the man by his given name for the first time, "you remember the time it took me four hours to find that bottle of rocket juice you hid on that old Titan freighter?"

Shinny cackled, his thin voice coming over the headphones of the others as well as Connel's.

"I sure do, Lou!" replied Shinny, using Connel's first name. They were just old spacemen now, reliving old times together. "Funny thing, though, you never knew I had two more bottles hidden in the tube chamber!"

"Why, you old space crawler!" roared Connel. "You put one over on me!"

Roger and Astro and Alfie had never known Connel's first name. They rolled the name over in their minds, fitting the name to the man. Unknown to each other, they decided that the name fitted the man. Lou Connel!

"Say, Lou," asked Shinny, "where in the blessed universe did you come from? You never told me."

There was a long pause. "A place called Telfair Estates, in the deep South on the North American continent. I was raised on a farm close by. I used to go fishing late at night and stare up at the stars." He paused again. "I ran away from home. I don't know if—if—anyone's still there or not. I never went back!"

There was a long silence as each man saw a small boy fishing late at night, bare-foot, his toes dangling in the water, a worm wiggling on the end of a string, more interested in the stars that twinkled overhead than in any fish that might swim past and seize the hook.

"Where are you from, Nick?" asked Connel.

"Born in space," cackled Shinny, "on a passenger freighter carrying colonists out to Titan. Never had a breath of natural fresh air until I was almost a grown man. Nothing but synthetic stuff under the atmosphere screens. My father was a mining engineer. I was the only kid. One night a screen busted and nearly everybody suffocated or froze to death. My pa and ma was among 'em. I blasted off after that. Been in the deep ever since. And you know, by the blessed rings of Saturn, I'd be on a nice farm near Venusport, living on a pension, if you hadn't kicked me out of the Solar Guard!"

"Why, you broken down old piece of space junk," roared Connel, "I oughta—" Connel never finished what he was going to say.

"Attention! Attention! Roger—Astro—Major Connel—come in, please! This is Tom on the *Polaris*!"

As if they had been struck by a bolt of lightning, the five spacemen sat up and then raced to the jet boat.

"Connel to Corbett!" roared the major. "Where are you? What happened?"

"I haven't got time to explain now, sir," said Tom. "Loring and Mason escaped and forced me to take them to Tara. I managed to overcome them and blast back here. Meet me up about fifty miles above Junior, sir. I'm bringing the *Polaris* in!"

"No!" yelled Connel. "It's no use, Tom. We're out of fuel. We've used up all our power."

"Then stand by," said Tom grimly. "I'm coming in for a landing!"

"No, Tom!" roared Connel. "There's nothing you can do. We're too far into the sun's pull. You'll never blast off again!"

"I don't care if we all wind up as cinders," said Tom, "I'm coming in!"

The communicator went dead and from the left, over the close horizon of the small satellite, the *Polaris* swept into view like a red-tailed fire dragon. It shot up in a pretouchdown maneuver, and then began to drop slowly to the surface of the planetoid.

No sooner had the *Polaris* touched the dry airless ground than the air-lock hatch was opened. From the crystal port on the control deck, Tom waved to the men below him.

Shinny climbed into the lock first, followed by Astro, Alfie, Roger, and Connel. While Roger and Alfie closed the hatch, Astro and Connel adjusted the oxygen pressure and waited for the supply to build to normal. At last the hissing stopped, and the hatch to the inner part of the ship opened. Tom greeted them with a smile and an outstretched hand.

"Glad to have you aboard!" he joked.

After the back slapping between Roger, Astro, and Tom was over, Connel questioned Tom on his strange departure from the satellite.

"It was just like I told you, sir," explained Tom. "They got out of the brig," he paused, not mentioning the spoon that Loring had used or how he had gotten it. "They forced me to take them to Tara. I managed to get the gravity turned off and gave them a lesson in free-fall fighting. They're still frozen stiff up on the control deck."

"Good boy!" said Connel. "I'll go and have a talk with them. Meantime, Astro, you and Shinny and Alfie get below and see how much fuel we have in emergency supply. We're going to need every ounce we have."

"Aye, aye, sir," said Astro. The three hurried to the power deck.

Connel followed Roger and Tom to the control deck. Loring and Mason were still in the positions they were in when Tom had fired his paralo-ray. Connel took Tom's gun and switched to the neutralizer. He fired twice and the two men rose shakily to their feet. Connel faced them, his eyes burning.

"I'm going to say very little to you two space-crawling rats!" snapped Connel. "I'm not going to lock you in the brig; I'm not going to confine you in any manner. But if you make one false move, I'll court-martial you right here and now! You've caused enough trouble with your selfishness, jeopardizing the lives of six men. If we fail to get off this satellite, it'll be because *you* put us in this position. Now get below and see what aid you can give Astro. And if either of you so much as raises your voice, I'm going to let *him* take care of you! Is that clear?"

"Yes, sir!" mumbled Loring. "We understand, sir. And we'll do everything we can to—to—make up for what we've done."

"The only thing you can do is to stay out of my sight!" said Connel coldly.

Loring and Mason scuttled past Connel and climbed down to the power deck.

"Attention! Attention! Control deck—Major Connel! Sir, this is Roger on the radar bridge. I just checked over Tom's figures on thrust, sir, and I'm not sure, but I think we've passed the point of safety."

"Thanks, Roger," said Connel. He turned to the intercom. "Power deck, check in!"

"Power deck, aye," said Astro.

"Loring and Mason there?" asked Connel.

"Yes, sir. I'm putting them right to work in the radiation chamber, sir. I'm piling all emergency fuel into the reaction chambers to try for one big push!"

"Why?" asked Connel.

"I heard what Roger said, sir," replied Astro. "This'll give us enough thrust to clear the sun's gravity, but there's something else that might not take it."

"What?" asked Connel.

"The cooling pumps, sir," said Astro. "They may not be able to handle a load as hot as this. We might blow up."

Connel considered this a moment. "Do what you can, Astro. I have absolute faith in you."

"Aye, aye, sir," said Astro. "And thank you. If this wagon holds together, I'll get her off."

Connel turned to Tom who stood ready at the control panel.

"All set, sir," said Tom. "Roger's given me a clear trajectory forward and up. All we need is Astro's push!"

"Unless Astro can build enough pressure in those cooling pumps to handle the overload of reactant fuel, we're done for. We'll get off this moon in pieces!"

"Power deck to control deck."

"Come in, Astro," said Tom.

"Almost ready, Tom," said Astro. "Maximum pressure is eight hundred and we're up to seven seventy now."

"Very well, Astro," replied Connel. "Let her build all the way to an even eight hundred and blast at my command."

"Aye, aye, sir," said Astro.

The mighty pumps on the power deck began their piercing shriek. Higher and higher they built up the pressure, until the ship began to rock under the strain.

"Stand by, Tom," ordered Connel, "and if you've ever twisted those dials, twist them now!"

"Yes, sir," replied Tom.

"Pressure up to seven ninety-one, sir," reported Astro.

"Attention! All members strap into acceleration cushions!"

One by one, Shinny and Alfie, Loring and Mason, Astro and Roger strapped themselves into the acceleration cushions. Roger set the radar scanner and strapped himself in on the radar bridge. Connel slumped into the second pilot's chair and took over the controls of the ship, strapping himself in, while Tom beside him did the same. The whine of the pumps was now a shrill whistle that drowned out all other sounds, and the great ship bucked under the force of the thrust building in her heart.

In front of the power-deck control panel Astro watched the pressure gauge mount steadily.

"Pressure up to seven ninety-six, sir," he called.

"Stand by to fire all rockets!" roared Connel.

"Make it good, you Venusian clunk," yelled Roger.

"Seven ninety-nine, sir!" bellowed Astro.

Astro watched the gauge of the pressure creep slowly toward the eight-hundred mark. In all his experience he had never seen it above seven hundred. Shinny, too, his merry eyes shining bright, watched the needle jerk back and forth and finally reach the eight-hundred mark.

"Eight hundred, sir," bellowed Astro.

"Fire all stern rockets!" roared Connel.

Astro threw the switch. On the control board, Connel saw a red light flash on. He jammed the master switch down hard.

It was the last thing he remembered.

CHAPTER 21

Tom stirred. He rolled his head from side to side. His mouth was dry and there was a sick feeling in the pit of his stomach. He opened his eyes and stared at the control panel in front of him. Instinctively he began to check the dials and gauges. He settled on one and waited for his pounding heart to return to normal. His eyes cleared, and the gauge swam into view. He read the figures aloud:

"Distance in miles since departure—fourteen thousand, five hundred ..."

Something clicked. He let out a yell.

"We made it! We made it!" He turned and began to pound Connel on the back. "Major Connel! Major, wake up, sir! We made it. We're in free fall! Junior's far behind us!"

"Uh—ah—what—Tom? What?" Connel said, rolling his eyes. In all his experience he had never felt such acceleration. He glanced at the gauge.

"Distance," he read, "fifteen thousand miles." The gauge ticked on.

"We made it, sir!" said Tom. "Astro gave us a kick in the pants we'll never forget!"

Connel grinned at Tom's excitement. There was reason to be excited. They were free. He turned to the intercom, but before he could speak, Astro's voice roared into his ears.

"Report from the power deck, sir," said Astro. "Acceleration normal. Request permission to open up on hyperdrive."

"Permission granted!" said Connel.

"Look, sir," said Tom, "on the teleceiver screen. Junior is getting his bumps!"

Connel glanced up at the screen. One by one the white puffs of dust from the reactor units were exploding on the surface of the planetoid. Soon the whole satellite was covered with the radioactive cloud.

"I'm sure glad we're not on that baby now," whispered Tom.

"Same here, spaceman!" said Connel.

It was evening of the first full day after leaving Junior before the routine of the long haul back to Space Academy had begun. The ***Polaris*** was on automatic control, and everyone was assembled in the messroom.

"Well, boys," said Connel, "our mission is a complete success. I've finished making out a report to Space Academy, and everything's fine. Incidentally, Manning," he continued, "if you're worried about having broken your word when you escaped from the space station, forget it. You more than made up for it by your work in helping us get Loring and Mason."

Roger smiled gratefully and gulped, "Thank you, sir."

Loring and Mason, who had eaten their meal separately from the others, listened silently. Loring got up and faced them. The room became silent.

Loring flushed.

"I'd like to say something," he began haltingly, "if I can?"

"Go ahead," said Connel.

"Well," said Loring, "it's hard to say this, but Mason and myself, well—" He paused. "I don't know what happened to us on the first trip out here, Major, but when we saw that satellite, and the copper, something just went wrong inside. One thing led to another, and before we knew it, we were in so deep we couldn't get out."

The faces around the table were stony, expressionless.

"Nobody deserves less consideration than me and Mason. And—well, you know yourself, sir, that we were pretty good spacemen at one time. You picked us for the first trip out to Tara with you."

Connel nodded.

"And well, sir, the main thing is about Jardine and Bangs. I know we're going to be sent to the prison asteroid and we deserve it. But we been thinking, sir, about Jardine's and Bang's wives and kids. They musta lost everything in that crash of the ***Annie Jones***, so if the major would recommend that Mason and me be sent to the Titan mines, instead of the rock, we could send our credits back to help take care of the kids and all."

"I know we're going to be sent to the prison asteroid and we deserve it,"
said Loring.

No one spoke.

"That's all," said Loring. He and Mason left the room.

Connel glanced around the table. "Well?" he asked. "This is your first struggle with justice. Each of you, Tom, Roger, Astro, Alfie, will be faced with this sort of thing during your careers as spacemen. What would you do?"

The four cadets looked at each other, each wondering what the other would say. Finally Connel turned to Alfie.

"You're first, Alfie," said Connel.

"I'd send them to the mines, sir," said Alfie.

Connel's face was impressive. "Roger?"

"Same here, sir," replied Roger.

"Astro?" asked Connel.

"I'd do anything to help the kids, sir," said Astro, an orphan himself.

"Tom?"

Tom hesitated. "They deserve the rock, sir. I don't have any feeling for them. But if they go to the rock, that doesn't do any more than punish them. If they go to the mines, they'll be punished and help someone else too. I'd send them to Titan and exile them from Earth forever."

Connel studied the cadets a moment. He turned to Shinny.

"Think they made a good decision, Nick?"

"I like what young Tommy, here, had to say, Lou," answered Shinny. "Best part about justice is when the man himself suffers from his own guilty feelings, rather than what you do to him as punishment. I think they did all right!"

"All right," said Connel. "I'll make the recommendation as you have suggested." Suddenly he turned to Shinny. "What about you in all this, Nick? I don't mean that you were hooked up with Loring and Mason. I know you were just prospecting and you've proved yourself to be a true spaceman. But what will happen to you now?"

"I'll tell you what's going to happen to me," snapped Shinny. "You're going to re-enlist me in the Solar Guard, right here! Right now!"

"What?" exploded Connel.

"And then you're going to retire me, right here, right now, with a full pension!"

"Why you old space-crawling—" Suddenly he looked around the table and saw the laughing faces of Tom, Roger, Astro, and Alfie.

"All right," he said, "but between your enlistment and your retirement, I'm going to make you polish every bit of brass on this space wagon, from the radar mast to the exhaust tubes!"

Shinny smiled his toothless smile and looked at Tom.

"Get the logbook, Tommy," he said. "This is official. I'm going to do something no other man in the entire history of the Solar Guard ever did before!"

"What's that, Mr. Shinny?" asked Tom with a smile.

"Enlist, serve time, and retire with a full pension, all on the same blasted spaceship, the *Polaris*!"

THE END

The Codes Of Hammurabi And Moses
W. W. Davies

QTY

The discovery of the Hammurabi Code is one of the greatest achievements of archaeology, and is of paramount interest, not only to the student of the Bible, but also to all those interested in ancient history...

Religion   **ISBN:** *1-59462-338-4*   **Pages:132**

MSRP $12.95

The Theory of Moral Sentiments
Adam Smith

QTY

This work from 1749. contains original theories of conscience amd moral judgment and it is the foundation for systemof morals.

Philosophy **ISBN:** *1-59462-777-0*   **Pages:536**

MSRP $19.95

Jessica's First Prayer
Hesba Stretton

QTY

In a screened and secluded corner of one of the many railway-bridges which span the streets of London there could be seen a few years ago, from five o'clock every morning until half past eight, a tidily set-out coffee-stall, consisting of a trestle and board, upon which stood two large tin cans, with a small fire of charcoal burning under each so as to keep the coffee boiling during the early hours of the morning when the work-people were thronging into the city on their way to their daily toil...

Pages:84

Childrens   **ISBN:** *1-59462-373-2*   *MSRP $9.95*

My Life and Work
Henry Ford

QTY

Henry Ford revolutionized the world with his implementation of mass production for the Model T automobile. Gain valuable business insight into his life and work with his own auto-biography... "We have only started on our development of our country we have not as yet, with all our talk of wonderful progress, done more than scratch the surface. The progress has been wonderful enough but..."

Pages:300

Biographies/   **ISBN:** *1-59462-198-5*   *MSRP $21.95*

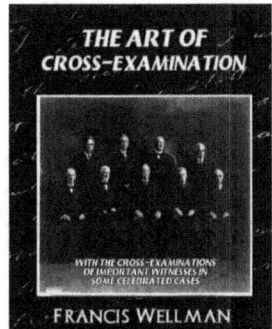

The Art of Cross-Examination
Francis Wellman

QTY

I presume it is the experience of every author, after his first book is published upon an important subject, to be almost overwhelmed with a wealth of ideas and illustrations which could readily have been included in his book, and which to his own mind, at least, seem to make a second edition inevitable. Such certainly was the case with me; and when the first edition had reached its sixth impression in five months, I rejoiced to learn that it seemed to my publishers that the book had met with a sufficiently favorable reception to justify a second and considerably enlarged edition. ...

Reference   ISBN: *1-59462-647-2*

Pages:412
MSRP $19.95

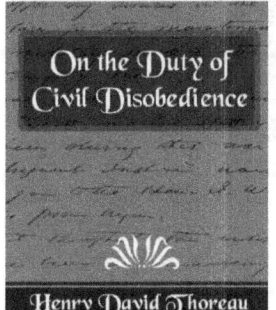

On the Duty of Civil Disobedience
Henry David Thoreau

QTY

Thoreau wrote his famous essay, On the Duty of Civil Disobedience, as a protest against an unjust but popular war and the immoral but popular institution of slave-owning. He did more than write—he declined to pay his taxes, and was hauled off to gaol in consequence. Who can say how much this refusal of his hastened the end of the war and of slavery ?

Law   ISBN: *1-59462-747-9*

Pages:48
MSRP $7.45

Dream Psychology Psychoanalysis for Beginners
Sigmund Freud

QTY

Sigmund Freud, born Sigismund Schlomo Freud (May 6, 1856 - September 23, 1939), was a Jewish-Austrian neurologist and psychiatrist who co-founded the psychoanalytic school of psychology. Freud is best known for his theories of the unconscious mind, especially involving the mechanism of repression; his redefinition of sexual desire as mobile and directed towards a wide variety of objects; and his therapeutic techniques, especially his understanding of transference in the therapeutic relationship and the presumed value of dreams as sources of insight into unconscious desires.

Psychology   ISBN: *1-59462-905-6*

Pages:196
MSRP $15.45

The Miracle of Right Thought
Orison Swett Marden

QTY

Believe with all of your heart that you will do what you were made to do. When the mind has once formed the habit of holding cheerful, happy, prosperous pictures, it will not be easy to form the opposite habit. It does not matter how improbable or how far away this realization may see, or how dark the prospects may be, if we visualize them as best we can, as vividly as possible, hold tenaciously to them and vigorously struggle to attain them, they will gradually become actualized, realized in the life. But a desire, a longing without endeavor, a yearning abandoned or held indifferently will vanish without realization.

Self Help   ISBN: *1-59462-644-8*

Pages:360
MSRP $25.45

www.**bookjungle**.com *email: sales@bookjungle.com fax: 630-214-0564 mail: Book Jungle PO Box 2226 Champaign, IL 61825*

QTY

The Rosicrucian Cosmo-Conception Mystic Christianity by *Max Heindel* ISBN: *1-59462-188-8* **$38.95**
The Rosicrucian Cosmo-conception is not dogmatic, neither does it appeal to any other authority than the reason of the student. It is: not controversial, but is: sent forth in the, hope that it may help to clear... New Age/Religion Pages 646

Abandonment To Divine Providence by *Jean-Pierre de Caussade* ISBN: *1-59462-228-0* **$25.95**
"The Rev. Jean Pierre de Caussade was one of the most remarkable spiritual writers of the Society of Jesus in France in the 18th Century. His death took place at Toulouse in 1751. His works have gone through many editions and have been republished... Inspirational/Religion Pages 400

Mental Chemistry by *Charles Haanel* ISBN: *1-59462-192-6* **$23.95**
Mental Chemistry allows the change of material conditions by combining and appropriately utilizing the power of the mind. Much like applied chemistry creates something new and unique out of careful combinations of chemicals the mastery of mental chemistry... New Age/Business Pages 354

The Letters of Robert Browning and Elizabeth Barret Barrett 1845-1846 vol II ISBN: *1-59462-193-4* **$35.95**
by *Robert Browning* and *Elizabeth Barrett* Biographies Pages 596

Gleanings In Genesis (volume I) by *Arthur W. Pink* ISBN: *1-59462-130-6* **$27.45**
Appropriately has Genesis been termed "the seed plot of the Bible" for in it we have, in germ form, almost all of the great doctrines which are afterwards fully developed in the books of Scripture which follow... Religion Pages 420

The Master Key by *L. W. de Laurence* ISBN: *1-59462-001-6* **$30.95**
In no branch of human knowledge has there been a more lively increase of the spirit of research during the past few years than in the study of Psychology, Concentration and Mental Discipline. The requests for authentic lessons in Thought Control, Mental Discipline and... New Age Pages 422

The Lesser Key Of Solomon Goetia by *L. W. de Laurence* ISBN: *1-59462-092-X* **$9.95**
This translation of the first book of the "Lemegton" which is now for the first time made accessible to students of Talismanic Magic was done, after careful collation and edition, from numerous Ancient Manuscripts in Hebrew, Latin, and French... New Age/Occult Pages 92

Rubaiyat Of Omar Khayyam by *Edward Fitzgerald* ISBN:*1-59462-332-5* **$13.95**
Edward Fitzgerald, whom the world has already learned, in spite of his own efforts to remain within the shadow of anonymity, to look upon as one of the rarest poets of the century, was born at Bredfield, in Suffolk, on the 31st of March, 1809. He was the third son of John Purcell... Music Pages 172

Ancient Law by *Henry Maine* ISBN: *1-59462-128-4* **$29.95**
The chief object of the following pages is to indicate some of the earliest ideas of mankind, as they are reflected in Ancient Law, and to point out the relation of those ideas to modern thought. Religiom/History Pages 452

Far-Away Stories by *William J. Locke* ISBN: *1-59462-129-2* **$19.45**
"Good wine needs no bush, but a collection of mixed vintages does. And this book is just such a collection. Some of the stories I do not want to remain buried for ever in the museum files of dead magazine-numbers an author's not unpardonable vanity..." Fiction Pages 272

Life of David Crockett by *David Crockett* ISBN: *1-59462-250-7* **$27.45**
"Colonel David Crockett was one of the most remarkable men of the times in which he lived. Born in humble life, but gifted with a strong will, an indomitable courage, and unremitting perseverance... Biographies/New Age Pages 424

Lip-Reading by *Edward Nitchie* ISBN: *1-59462-206-X* **$25.95**
Edward B. Nitchie, founder of the New York School for the Hard of Hearing, now the Nitchie School of Lip-Reading, Inc, wrote "LIP-READING Principles and Practice". The development and perfecting of this meritorious work on lip-reading was an undertaking... How-to Pages 400

A Handbook of Suggestive Therapeutics, Applied Hypnotism, Psychic Science ISBN: *1-59462-214-0* **$24.95**
by *Henry Munro* Health/New Age/Health/Self-help Pages 376

A Doll's House: and Two Other Plays by *Henrik Ibsen* ISBN: *1-59462-112-8* **$19.95**
Henrik Ibsen created this classic when in revolutionary 1848 Rome. Introducing some striking concepts in playwriting for the realist genre, this play has been studied the world over. Fiction/Classics/Plays 308

The Light of Asia by *sir Edwin Arnold* ISBN: *1-59462-204-3* **$13.95**
In this poetic masterpiece, Edwin Arnold describes the life and teachings of Buddha. The man who was to become known as Buddha to the world was born as Prince Gautama of India but he rejected the worldly riches and abandoned the reigns of power when... Religion/History/Biographies Pages 170

The Complete Works of Guy de Maupassant by *Guy de Maupassant* ISBN: *1-59462-157-8* **$16.95**
"For days and days, nights and nights, I had dreamed of that first kiss which was to consecrate our engagement, and I knew not on what spot I should put my lips..." Fiction/Classics Pages 240

The Art of Cross-Examination by *Francis L. Wellman* ISBN: *1-59462-309-0* **$26.95**
Written by a renowned trial lawyer, Wellman imparts his experience and uses case studies to explain how to use psychology to extract desired information through questioning. How-to/Science/Reference Pages 408

Answered or Unanswered? by *Louisa Vaughan* ISBN: *1-59462-248-5* **$10.95**
Miracles of Faith in China Religion Pages 112

The Edinburgh Lectures on Mental Science (1909) by *Thomas* ISBN: *1-59462-008-3* **$11.95**
This book contains the substance of a course of lectures recently given by the writer in the Queen Street Hall, Edinburgh. Its purpose is to indicate the Natural Principles governing the relation between Mental Action and Material Conditions... New Age/Psychology Pages 148

Ayesha by *H. Rider Haggard* ISBN: *1-59462-301-5* **$24.95**
Verily and indeed it is the unexpected that happens! Probably if there was one person upon the earth from whom the Editor of this, and of a certain previous history, did not expect to hear again... Classics Pages 380

Ayala's Angel by *Anthony Trollope* ISBN: *1-59462-352-X* **$29.95**
The two girls were both pretty, but Lucy who was twenty-one who supposed to be simple and comparatively unattractive, whereas Ayala was credited, as her Bombwhat romantic name might show, with poetic charm and a taste for romance. Ayala when her father died was nineteen... Fiction Pages 484

The American Commonwealth by *James Bryce* ISBN: *1-59462-286-8* **$34.45**
An interpretation of American democratic political theory. It examines political mechanics and society from the perspective of Scotsman James Bryce Politics Pages 572

Stories of the Pilgrims by *Margaret P. Pumphrey* ISBN: *1-59462-116-0* **$17.95**
This book explores pilgrims religious oppression in England as well as their escape to Holland and eventual crossing to America on the Mayflower, and their early days in New England... History Pages 268

QTY

The Fasting Cure *by Sinclair Upton* ISBN: *1-59462-222-1* **$13.95**
In the Cosmopolitan Magazine for May, 1910, and in the Contemporary Review (London) for April, 1910, I published an article dealing with my experiences in fasting. I have written a great many magazine articles, but never one which attracted so much attention... New Age/Self Help/Health Pages 164

Hebrew Astrology *by Sepharial* ISBN: *1-59462-308-2* **$13.45**
In these days of advanced thinking it is a matter of common observation that we have left many of the old landmarks behind and that we are now pressing forward to greater heights and to a wider horizon than that which represented the mind-content of our progenitors... Astrology Pages 144

Thought Vibration or The Law of Attraction in the Thought World ISBN: *1-59462-127-6* **$12.95**
by William Walker Atkinson *Psychology/Religion Pages 144*

Optimism *by Helen Keller* ISBN: *1-59462-108-X* **$15.95**
Helen Keller was blind, deaf, and mute since 19 months old, yet famously learned how to overcome these handicaps, communicate with the world, and spread her lectures promoting optimism. An inspiring read for everyone... Biographies/Inspirational Pages 84

Sara Crewe *by Frances Burnett* ISBN: *1-59462-360-0* **$9.45**
In the first place, Miss Minchin lived in London. Her home was a large, dull, tall one, in a large, dull square, where all the houses were alike, and all the sparrows were alike, and where all the door-knockers made the same heavy sound... Childrens/Classic Pages 88

The Autobiography of Benjamin Franklin *by Benjamin Franklin* ISBN: *1-59462-135-7* **$24.95**
The Autobiography of Benjamin Franklin has probably been more extensively read than any other American historical work, and no other book of its kind has had such ups and downs of fortune. Franklin lived for many years in England, where he was agent... Biographies/History Pages 332

Name	
Email	
Telephone	
Address	
City, State ZIP	

☐ **Credit Card**   ☐ **Check / Money Order**

Credit Card Number	
Expiration Date	
Signature	

Please Mail to: Book Jungle
PO Box 2226
Champaign, IL 61825
or Fax to: *630-214-0564*

ORDERING INFORMATION

web: *www.bookjungle.com*
email: *sales@bookjungle.com*
fax: *630-214-0564*
mail: *Book Jungle PO Box 2226 Champaign, IL 61825*
or PayPal *to sales@bookjungle.com*

Please contact us for bulk discounts

DIRECT-ORDER TERMS

**20% Discount if You Order
Two or More Books**
Free Domestic Shipping!
Accepted: Master Card, Visa,
Discover, American Express